MH

BOOKS BY CAROL HIGGINS CLARK

Cursed

Zapped

Laced

Hitched

Burned

Popped

Jinxed

Fleeced

Twanged

Iced

Snagged

Decked

WITH MARY HIGGINS CLARK

Dashing Through the Snow

Santa Cruise

The Christmas Thief

He Sees You When You're Sleeping

Deck the Halls

CAROL HIGGINS CLARK

WRECKED

A Regan Reilly Mystery

SCRIBNER

New York   London   Toronto   Sydney

SCRIBNER
A Division of Simon & Schuster, Inc.
1230 Avenue of the Americas
New York, NY 10020

This Scribner export edition April 2010

SCRIBNER and design are registered trademarks of The Gale Group, Inc.,
used under license by Simon & Schuster, Inc., the publisher of this work.

For information about special discounts for bulk purchases,
please contact Simon & Schuster Special Sales at
1-866-506-1949 or business@simonandschuster.com.

The Simon & Schuster Speakers Bureau can bring authors
to your live event. For more information or to book an event,
contact the Simon & Schuster Speakers Bureau at
1-866-248-3049 or visit our website at www.simonspeakers.com.

Designed by Carla Jones

Manufactured in the United States of America

1 3 5 7 9 10 8 6 4 2

ISBN 978-1-4391-8412-7

Acknowledgments

I would like to thank the following people for getting *Wrecked*— through its journey to publication.

A very special thanks to my editor, Roz Lippel. I am so grateful for her constant hard work, wonderful guidance, and best of all, her dedication to my books. Thank you, Roz! I couldn't have a better person at the helm!

Associate Director of Copyediting Gypsy da Silva.

Scribner Publishing Manager Kara Watson.

Scribner Art Director Rex Bonomelli.

Senior Production Manager Lisa Erwin.

Copyeditor Anne Cherry.

Proofreader Ted Landry.

Designer Carla Jones.

My publicist, Lisl Cade.

My agent, Esther Newberg.

My mother, Mary Higgins Clark, my aunt Irene Clark, and the rest of my family and friends who saw me through the storm.

The sun's out now! Thank you all!

In memory of Denis J. Carey III
"DJ"
Whose multitude of friends remember him with joy

DJ—New York City isn't the same without you!

WRECKED

Friday, April 7th

1

Regan Reilly shivered as she padded around the kitchen of her in-laws' summer home. Outside, the wind was howling. Sheets of rain pelted against the house. At the sink Regan stopped and stared out the window. As far as the eye could see, whitecaps churned in the waters of Cape Cod Bay.

Regan pulled her terry-cloth bathrobe more tightly around her waist and smiled. I love this weather, she thought. There's nothing like riding out a storm in a house like this. She and her husband, Jack, had driven up from Manhattan the night before to spend a quiet weekend in celebration of their first wedding anniversary. Arriving just as the bad weather started, they'd lit a fire in the den, poured glasses of wine, and enjoyed the basket of sandwiches and fruit and cheese Regan had prepared for the trip. They relished being alone and just doing as they pleased for the next three days. The only big plans they had were to go out for dinner on Sunday night to an award-winning restaurant on the water that had been converted from an old captain's house and served only twelve meals a night. Apparently the chef could get a little cranky if he was asked to cook a morsel more.

The coffeemaker on the counter hissed and sputtered, firing the last few drops of freshly brewed java into the waiting carafe. That sounds so loud, Regan thought. You'd never even hear it during the summer, when the house was overflowing with Jack's brothers and sisters and nieces and nephews and assorted family friends—there was so much activity. Conversation filled the air. Someone was always attempting to tell a story or a joke without interruption. Few were successful. The days were filled with swimming and waterskiing and firing up the grill. In the evenings, everyone would gather on the big deck to watch the sunset. Thirty-nine steps down from the deck was the beach where Jack and his brothers often anchored the powerboat that they'd brought over from its spot at the marina. What a difference, Regan mused. Except for the wind and the rain and the creaking of the house and the coffeepot, this place is so quiet!

Regan poured coffee into a mug, then reached for the refrigerator door and pulled it open. She grabbed the container of skim milk that Skip the caretaker had stocked for them. Jack's mother was in regular contact with him. A few days ago she asked him to bring in milk and juice and butter and bread when he did his weekly check on the house. Just enough for Regan and Jack to have breakfast on their first morning. The coffee smells great, Regan thought. I can't wait to sit in the den with this cup and watch the storm. She poured the milk into the mug and stared in horror as it curdled. What? How can that be? She checked the expiration date. The milk had expired two weeks ago. Did he bring this from home? Regan wondered as she woefully poured her coffee down the sink.

Jack, freshly showered, appeared in the kitchen. "I'll run up to the market and get the papers," he said.

Regan turned to him and smiled. He looked so handsome. Jack was six foot two, with hazel eyes and sandy hair. He was wearing jeans and a windbreaker. "Put milk on your list."

"I thought Skip brought in milk for us."

"He did. Only trouble is, he managed to produce a container that expired two weeks ago."

Jack laughed. "That kid is unbelievable. I don't know why my mother doesn't fire him."

"That'll never happen," Regan said. "His little-boy-lost quality has made your mother feel very maternal and protective of him."

Jack shook his head, leaned down to give Regan a kiss, and put his arms around her. "I'll pick up some muffins. I'm not trusting that anything he bought for us is edible." He hugged Regan tight. "It's so great to be here alone with you. No work to distract us."

Jack was head of the NYPD Major Case Squad. Regan was a private investigator. They had both been busy with cases that thankfully wrapped up in the past few days.

"It is going to be a wonderful weekend," Regan said as Jack released her. "I'll jump in the shower and look forward to your return."

Jack laughed. "What you really want is for me to hurry back with the milk so you can have your first cup of coffee."

"You know me so well," Regan murmured as Jack headed for the front door.

In the downstairs master bathroom, Regan turned on the shower. The hot water felt so good on her shoulders and back. A few minutes later she pulled a pair of jeans and a sweater out of her suitcase on the bedroom floor. I don't think I've ever been alone in this house, she thought. So why don't I feel alone? She dressed, brushed her dark hair, then started to apply makeup to her pale skin. With her blue eyes, she fell into the category of "Black Irish."

It might not be sunny outside, but I need more light, Regan thought. She stepped over to the window, fumbled for the cord, then gave it a yank. The curtains flew open.

A man in a yellow hooded slicker had his nose pressed against the glass.

Regan screamed.

It was Skip. He stumbled back. "Sorry!" he yelled.

Regan couldn't hear the rest of what he was saying. She turned the handle of the window, which opened out.

"Sorry!" Skip yelled again through the roaring wind. "I was just checking the drainpipes."

I'll bet, Regan thought. "You startled me," she said, her heart beating wildly.

"I didn't mean to. This storm caused a lot of damage on the Cape. I'd like to come in and check all the windows and the basement. Make sure there are no leaks or anything." He smiled up at Regan. Curls of brown hair escaped from the hood of his rain gear.

His face was the picture of innocence, but Regan felt un-nerved. "Okay," she said, wanting to ask him how he managed to buy expired milk.

"I'll check the other drainpipes then come on in," Skip said, waving his hands. "You can't be too careful, you know."

"No you can't," Regan agreed as she cranked the window shut. Jack's mother had joked that the minute Skip came into the house he never stopped talking. Months of living alone up here in the wintertime took its toll. When he finally got an audi-ence, he never let them go. Well, Regan thought, her heart still racing, I'm sure Jack can handle it. I wish he were here right now.

The sound of the front door opening flooded her with relief. "Regan?" Jack called.

Thank God, Regan thought as she raced out of the bedroom and down the hall. "Jack, I'm so glad you're back!"

When she got to the living room, she stopped short. The two gossipy women who lived in the house three doors down were standing with Jack. Regan couldn't think of their names but knew that they were sisters. They were like a double dose of Mrs. Kravitz, the quintessential nosy neighbor on the old TV series *Bewitched*.

"Gee, you two are like newlyweds," one of them cackled. "Look at the way you run and greet your husband when he only was gone a few minutes buying the newspaper."

"Jack tells us it's your first anniversary," the other chimed in. "The way you act, it seems more like you got married yesterday."

Regan managed a smile. "I was just worried with him being out in this storm. I understand it's done quite a bit of damage."

"Oh, you're right about that, Regan," the taller sister said. "A huge branch snapped off the big tree in our yard and came crashing through our front window. What a mess! We flagged Jack down when he was coming back from the market. He pulled the branch out of the way, then covered the hole with plastic. There's glass all over our living room. We asked if we could stay at your place until things are back to normal. Ginny and I both feel as if we're coming down with colds as it is. Now our house is a drafty mess. You don't mind, do you? Jack's mother has been such a dear to us over the years."

I don't believe this, Regan thought. This can't be happening. All our weekend plans. "Of course I don't mind," she finally croaked, stealing a glance at Jack, who raised his eyebrows in despair. He looked as if he were about to go through the floor.

"You're so kind, Regan. Thank you. There's nothing like neighbors you can call on in a time of need." She sniffed the air.

"That coffee smells great to me. Did you make that yourself, Regan?"

"Yes, I did."

"I wouldn't mind a cup. But I only take it with skim milk. Doctor's orders."

"We've got plenty of skim milk," Jack said, holding up the grocery bag as they headed to the kitchen.

"Wonderful. Ginny and I want to hear all about your married bliss. But first I'd like to use your phone. I was trying to reach the window company from our house but had no luck. Something tells me it's going to take a good bit of time before we're back to normal."

Jack turned to Regan and mouthed one word: *Bermuda*.

It was the only other place they had considered going for their anniversary.

2

In Regan's childhood home in Summit, New Jersey, her parents, Nora and Luke, were just finishing breakfast. Luke, the owner of three funeral homes, was about to head to work. Nora, a well-known suspense writer, would then go up to her third floor office to work on her latest novel.

"I can't believe it was this very weekend last year that Regan and Jack got married," Nora said wistfully as she folded the newspaper. "I wish we could do that day all over again."

"Just as long as they don't send us the bill," Luke muttered as he pushed his chair back from the kitchen table.

"No father was prouder than you walking his daughter down the aisle."

"True," Luke responded. "But if I want to relive that day, I'll go to the videotape." He stood, his six-foot-five-inch lanky frame encased in a dark suit, white shirt, and subdued tie. With his silver hair and handsome face, he looked quite distinguished.

Nora glanced out the window at the driving rain. "We were blessed with a beautiful sunny day last year. Anyone getting married this weekend better not have their heart set on outdoor photos."

"I'm sure there are plenty of grooms out there right now

wringing their hands at the thought of no pictures in the garden."

"You're impossible." Nora laughed as she started to clear the plates from the table. Standing next to Luke, she seemed absolutely petite. Five foot three inches tall, she had blond hair and fair skin that gave her a patrician look. Regan had inherited her height and coloring from Luke's side of the family. "I suppose Regan and Jack made it safely to the Cape."

"I'm sure we would have heard if they ran into any problems." Luke leaned down to give his wife a kiss. "Don't call them."

"I wasn't planning to," Nora protested. "I just hope this storm doesn't cause problems with FedEx."

Luke looked puzzled. "Why your sudden interest in the well-being of FedEx?"

"I forgot to give Regan the top layer of her wedding cake when she and Jack were here the other night."

"Her wedding cake? Isn't it stale by now?"

"Hopefully not. It's been in the freezer in the basement for the last year. There's an old tradition that says if a couple eats a slice of their wedding cake on their first anniversary, it will bring them good luck and is an omen for a long life."

"I don't recall us having wedding cake on our first anniversary."

"There wasn't any left. Your relatives polished off every last crumb at our reception."

"What?"

"A table of your cousins asked for seconds. Their waiter was young and inexperienced. He took it upon himself to cut up the extra cake that had been set aside for us to bring home."

"I like the sound of that guy," Luke said decisively, "someone who aims to please." He paused, his face baffled. "I just can't believe you never told me."

Nora batted her eyes. "I wasn't going to let anything ruin that day for us . . ."

Luke grinned. "Funny how times change. I'm certainly glad you've gotten over holding back about my relatives."

"I guess I have," Nora agreed. "And we've made it this far even though we didn't have wedding cake on our first anniversary. But I wasn't taking any chances for Regan and Jack. Yesterday, I FedExed the cake to Cape Cod."

Luke reached for his coat. "Let's hope the driver doesn't have a sweet tooth."

3

It wasn't long before Regan was able to figure out the names of their unexpected guests, the Brewer sisters. The older one was Fran, the younger Ginny. They both appeared to be in their sixties.

Fran was tall and thin, with big round glasses and wavy shoulder-length graying hair. Ginny, who did more talking than listening, was rounder, with frosted hair and wide brown eyes. She wore more makeup than Fran, but their outfits were similar—khaki pants, long-sleeved crewneck sweaters and all-weather shoes.

The minute they set foot in the kitchen, Fran had grabbed the cordless phone off the counter and started dialing. The window company's line was still busy. It took numerous tries before someone answered and promptly put Fran on hold.

"Wait!" she cried fruitlessly. "Darn it! It could take forever to talk to someone. I don't know how long that plastic is going to protect our living room if this wind and pelting rain keeps up. I need to get the window guys over here on the double." She leaned against the butcher-block counter and sighed.

"And what about getting rid of those branches that are all over the yard?" Ginny blurted as she slathered butter on the blueberry muffin that Jack had bought for Regan. She looked happy as a clam in her seat at the kitchen table. As Regan hungrily eyed her muffin, she tried to push away the thought that at this moment she and Jack could be enjoying room service in Bermuda.

"It's one big shame about our tree," Fran pronounced. "It'll be a heartbreaker if we have to cut it down. But first things first. We have to somehow take care of the window, then worry about everything else."

Ginny took a bite of the muffin. "Delicious," she pronounced, patting her mouth with a napkin. "Jack, your mother keeps a lovely home here. Just lovely. It's all so comfortable and inviting and"—she paused and rolled her eyes—"unlike the present state of our home, warm and toasty."

"Thank you," Jack answered.

Regan could tell he was doing his best to be cordial. *I think he's as shocked as I am that our weekend plans went down the drain so fast. I wonder if we could make an excuse and go back to New York.* Ginny had already mentioned that Jack's mother had let them stay here for a few days when their boiler blew last winter. *Or maybe we could go to Boston for the weekend. Heck, maybe we could find a no-tell motel somewhere between here and the Sagamore Bridge. Anywhere but here.*

"Fran and I just love the Cape," Ginny continued. "We can't believe we ended up here. Were we in shock three years ago when we found out our uncle had willed us his house!"

"My family never really knew him. He didn't spend much time here, did he?" Jack asked.

"No. He rented the house forever. That man was a character. Always on the run. He bought the house about ten years ago to use as a vacation home. Wouldn't you know, a month later he met his third wife whose lifelong dream was to live in Hawaii? He didn't want to sell the house so he began renting it out. The newlyweds moved to Maui, where he bought another beautiful home. He'd made this woman's dream come true, which made her happy for about five minutes. She turned out to be a nightmare. Within a year her next big desire was to get divorced. Once again Uncle Ned was thrilled to give her what she wanted. He even let her keep the house, which he'd paid for in cash. The day he signed the divorce papers, he got on a plane, wanting to put at least an ocean's distance between them. By then he'd grown quite fond of receiving fat checks from his tenants at the Cape house, so he didn't move here. He lived in Phoenix for a while, then Palm Beach. He had recently proposed to a woman who would become his fourth wife when he died in his sleep."

"Uncle Ned was an eternal optimist," Fran observed.

"And always so cheerful," Ginny added. "At the time he died, Fran and I were both getting ready to retire. We had a town house in Pennsylvania and didn't know where we wanted to spend our golden years. At first we thought the Cape might be too lonely in the wintertime. But we're doing our best to get to know people . . ."

No doubt, Regan thought.

Ginny pointed in the direction of the last house on the block. "Did you know that besides Mrs. Hopkins, the woman renting the Carpenters' place, we are the only people on this long lonely street in the dead of winter? Sad to say, our new neighbor is very unfriendly and doesn't seem to be interested in our company at all. I don't understand it. The day she moved in last November we brought over a homemade pie. Do you know she didn't even have the courtesy to invite us in? And she obviously doesn't believe in thank-you notes. Right, Fran?"

"I never saw one," Fran answered, impatiently tapping her fingers on the counter.

"It's not as if we hold it against her," Ginny said in a saintly tone. "We still always wave when she drives by, but she barely acknowledges us."

"Some people come up to the Cape to be alone," Jack replied. "I've never met her." He turned to Regan. "You said Skip is outside checking the drainpipes? Maybe I'll go out and help him."

He'd rather be outside in the driving rain than sit here with these two, Regan thought. "That's what Skip said he was going to do," she answered. "Who knows?"

Fran and Ginny glanced at each other. There was no doubt in Regan's mind that their exchange was an expression of disapproval about Skip.

"What?" Regan asked lightly, the carton of expired milk and Skip's appearance outside her window still fresh in her mind. "Do you two have something to tell us?"

"We should just mind our own business," Fran said unconvincingly.

"If there's something we should know . . ." Regan prodded.

Not surprisingly, Ginny pounced on the opportunity to gossip. "There *is* something you should know!" she declared, her eyes darting back and forth between Regan and Jack. "I always said that knowledge gives you power. And power gives you control. And control gives you—"

"Ginny!" Regan said with a laugh. "What should we know?"

Ginny cleared her throat. "Fran and I decided to take a walk on the beach a few weeks ago. It was the first day where you just felt spring was in the air. The only problem is that our stairs to the beach washed away in last year's big storm. Jack, your mother is the doll of dolls. She said we could use your staircase anytime. It's too much of an expense for us to fix ours on top of having to bring in more boulders to protect our land from all the erosion. Who thought a bunch of rocks could be so expensive? Anyway, Fran and I came down the road, walked by the side of

15

the house here, looked into the den, and there he was, Mr. Caretaker himself, sleeping on the couch with the television on. Is that his job?" she asked with a giggle. "To watch television?"

"I don't believe it's in the job description," Jack answered. "Maybe he was just taking a break."

"There's more!" Ginny exclaimed, obviously dissatisfied that Jack was letting Skip off the hook so easily. "After that we were on high alert. The next time we saw his car come down the road and park in your driveway, we decided to take another walk on the beach."

"Even though it was ten o'clock at night," Fran added, shifting the phone from one ear to the other. A maddening recording replayed endlessly, apologizing for the wait, then extolling the virtures of the window company.

"It was ten o'clock," Ginny agreed. "We were about to watch the local news but instead we got our coats on and walked down the road in the pitch dark. What we saw when we looked through these windows was mind-boggling. Skip was sitting right here in your den, drinking beer and watching a basketball game."

I bet the beer hadn't expired, Regan thought.

"Jack, I hope he doesn't charge your parents by the hour."

"I'll mention it to them," Jack said quickly.

"You should. After all, it doesn't seem right to take advantage of people like that." Ginny held up her mug. "Regan, is there any more coffee in the pot?"

"Oh . . . of course," Regan answered.

"Speak of the devil!" Fran crowed. "Look at what just washed ashore!"

All heads turned toward the den. Skip had just reached the top step from the beach and was racing toward the sliding glass doors. He looked frantic. Jack got up and hurried over to let him in. When he opened the door, the howling wind blew rain onto the tile floor.

Skip stumbled inside.

"Are you all right?" Jack asked as he forcefully pushed the door closed.

Water was dripping from Skip's slicker. His face and hair were soaked. He was breathing so heavily, he couldn't get any words out.

"Take it easy," Jack said, trying to comfort him.

The poor guy, Regan thought. Her heart went out to him. He was so completely distraught.

"What happened?" Fran demanded. It looked as if she was even tempted to hang up the phone.

"I wanted to check the staircase," Skip explained between breaths, "to make sure none of the steps were missing or loose. When I reached the bottom step, I looked over and saw Mrs. Hopkins's rowboat banging up against the rocks."

"She keeps a rowboat on the beach?" Jack asked.

"It's tied to the bottom of her staircase," Ginny yelled over, getting up from the table. "She likes to go out on the bay in that beat-up old thing at the craziest hours. It's so dangerous."

"Reminds me of *The Old Man and the Sea*," Fran chimed in.

Skip ignored them. "I went over to see if I could secure the boat for her. Mrs. Hopkins's body is in a heap at the bottom of her staircase!" he cried.

That did it. Fran hung up the phone.

"She's dead?" they were all asking at once.

"I think so, but I'm not sure. Her face is all bloody. Jack, we've got to get back down there!

Within a split second, the phone was back in Fran's hand. "I'll call nine-one-one!" she yelped as Regan and Jack grabbed their coats and hurried out the door with Skip.

4

At Fern's diner, a few miles from Jack's parents' home, the place was buzzing. Fern's clientele, especially the retired men, were not the type who liked to sit at home on a morning like this. As long as their roof wasn't about to cave in, they'd rather go out for a plate of pancakes and keep apprised of all the action around town. In the corner above the counter, a large flat-screen TV was tuned to a local Cape Cod station giving up-to-the-minute reports on downed trees, flooded roads, and power outages. When the words BREAKING NEWS flashed on-screen, people stopped talking and looked up at the TV expectantly. More often than not it was something mundane, like a reporter sorrowfully asking someone whose basement had flooded how they were feeling.

Storm or no storm, if you wanted to know about anything that was going on in the area, good, bad, or indifferent, all you had to do was show up at Fern's between the hours of 6 a.m. and 9 p.m.

Situated on a piece of land bordered on two sides by acres of grassy marshland and a meandering stream, a customer could glance out the window year after year at the same peaceful surroundings. Inside, it wasn't exactly peaceful, but there was just enough banter between the waitresses and the customers, and lively exchange among the tables, to give Fern's a friendly energy. Fern never played loud music that would drive out certain customers, and her staff was instructed to carefully place the dirty dishes and silverware in the rubber bins by the kitchen door. In many of the diners she had visited, the clatter of dishes and silverware being tossed around always rattled her nerves.

When Fern bought the spacious old building several years ago, she went to work transforming it into a cozy gathering spot. Homey flowered wallpaper and an assortment of kitchen tables and chairs secured at garage sales did the trick. The coffee was always hot, the food tasty, the prices fair. Best of all for those with laptops who wanted company around when they were working, there was wireless internet access. Worst of all for Fern was that these people were usually the types who stayed for hours on end and seemed to survive on coffee alone.

A sturdy muscular woman in her late thirties, Fern was the consummate, if slightly gruff, host. Her streaked blond hair always pulled back in a ponytail, she was always in motion. "What are ya having, hon?" she bellowed dozens of times a day. All year long the place was busy with locals stopping in for coffee or a meal. A group of retirees met there for breakfast every morning. Fern made it her business to greet everyone and glean some bit of personal information about any newcomers. At this time of year Fern and her customers were looking forward to the warm weather, even though some of the crowd begrudged the onslaught of tourists.

Today there was a table full of people Fern had never met before, a theater group called the Traveling Thespians. They had arrived in Chatwich late last night to start rehearsals for the play they'd be performing Memorial Day Weekend through the end of June. The owner of the famous Castle by the Sea, a mansion on the waterfront just down the road, had lent them the use of his property and his home. A tent would be erected on his vast lawn, to be used as the theater. Fern knew that tomorrow night they were having a cocktail party at the mansion to drum up excitement for their show. The only people who weren't happy about their presence were those who ran the long-established theater in town, Pilgrim's Playhouse, whose planks had been walked by many of the great stars of stage and screen. Privately they referred to the Traveling Thespians as the Traveling Hobos.

The founder of the Traveling Thespians, a man in his late fifties named Devon, called Fern over. When she arrived at the table, Fern tried not to stare at his hair. It was reddish brown with flecks of gray and seemed like a toupee, but then again it didn't. Fern had never seen anything like it. "We met ever so briefly when our group entered your wonderful establishment," Devon began in an exaggerated tone that set Fern's teeth on edge. If there was anything Fern couldn't stand, it was a pompous idiot. "You've heard about our party tomorrow night?" he asked.

"Yes, I have," Fern answered with a smile.

"I would just love it if you joined us as my guest. Bring a friend. It's going to be marvelous," he enthused. "Simply marrrrrvelous."

"I'll try," Fern said. "By the end of the day I'm pretty beat."

"But theater uplifts," Devon cried. "It renews one's spirit." He lowered his voice and paused dramatically. "The actors will be reading a scene from the play they'll be performing, a play that I wrote. I'm so thrilled to have the world premiere here on Cape Cod!"

A world premiere on someone's lawn? Fern thought. Give me a break. I should ask him if he'd like the world premiere of our next plate of eggs. And if this guy wrote the play, I know I won't like it. "I'll definitely try to get there," Fern replied, even sounding like she meant it. "Let's hope this storm lets up so you get a big crowd." She turned from the table and through the window saw a police cruiser pulling into the driveway. The cops in town were her friends, often spending their breaks at the first table by the counter, which was Fern's home base. There's no way they'll be taking breaks on a day like this, Fern thought. It'll be two coffees to go. But just as quickly as the cruiser pulled in, it did a U-turn, turned on its flashing lights, and sped out of the parking lot.

"Oh, Fern," Devon cried. "It looks like you just lost some business. But maybe something dramatic is happening! All the world's a stage . . ."

"Let's hope no one is hurt," Fern replied, trying not to sound annoyed. If this guy comes in here too often between now and the end of June, she thought, I'll definitely go crazy.

5

As Regan raced out the door behind Skip and Jack, she could see that the waves were now enormous. When Skip reached the stairs to the beach and looked down, he let out a howl.

"The waves are hitting the rocks!" he cried. "The beach is underwater! How could that have happened so fast?" He didn't wait for an answer.

The three of them made it down the slippery stairs as fast as possible. When they reached the bottom, they stepped into the freezing cold water, which was up to Regan's thighs. Turning to the right, they ran through the water as quickly as they could. Mrs. Hopkins's rowboat was now afloat, still banging against the rocks.

But Mrs. Hopkins was gone.

Skip became hysterical. "I left her right here," he yelled, kicking his feet in the water. "The tide must have pulled her out! We have to find her!" He started charging back and forth in the water near her staircase, apparently hoping he'd stumble over the body. Then he headed toward the deeper water, where the waves were breaking.

Jack grabbed his arm. "Skip, the undertow is very strong. I've never seen the bay this rough. If you go out there, you'll get pulled under. It's just too dangerous."

"But what about Mrs. Hopkins?" Skip asked as he broke into tears. "I never should have left her here."

Regan went over and put her arm around him. "Skip, it's not your fault."

Skip shook his head back and forth. "I guess I should have tried to pick her up and carry her up the steps."

"You couldn't have guessed that this would happen," Regan said.

Jack pulled his cell phone out of his pocket. "Fran was calling the police. I'm sure they'll be here soon. I'll call the coast guard."

Skip kicked the water. "I only wish I knew for sure that she was dead when I left her here! Because if she wasn't, then I'm responsible for her being dead now!"

Fran and Ginny ran to the front door the second they spotted a police car speeding down the block, its lights flashing. Two officers jumped out of the car.

"They're down on the beach," Ginny yelled out from the front porch. "Take the steps around the back. I didn't want to go down there. I've never seen a dead body before it was embalmed."

The officers ran around the side of the house. Within minutes another patrol car came racing down the block. They were also directed to the back of the house.

"Such excitement!" Ginny exclaimed to her sister as they stepped back inside. "I'd better make another pot of coffee."

"Good idea. I may as well give that window company another try. I'm sure our living room isn't getting any drier."

. . .

Jack recognized the policemen who were heading down to the beach, Officer Tom Barnes and Officer Jim Malone. He and Regan had met them the past summer at Fern's coffee shop. Quickly he apprised them of the situation.

"This woman rented the house right up here?" Barnes asked Skip.

"Yes."

"She lived alone?"

Skip shrugged. "I think so."

"That's the impression of our other neighbors who are up at my parents' house right now," Jack said. "None of us know much about her. My parents are friendly with the owners of the house she rented. We can contact them."

"Thanks, Jack. Had you met this woman?"

"No. Regan and I haven't been up to the Cape since she moved here."

Rain was pelting their faces. The icy water they were standing in was getting deeper.

Medics carrying a stretcher, firemen, and more police arrived. Searchers in hip boots started combing the beach, but the waves were getting bigger and the rain was coming down harder.

"This is too dangerous," Barnes decided. "We'll have to wait until the storm lets up to come back. I don't want anyone else getting pulled out by those currents. The coast guard will be on the lookout for the body." He called off the search, then turned to Skip. "If you don't mind, I'd just like to ask you a few more questions."

"Okay," Skip answered.

"Would you like to do the questioning at my parents' house?" Jack asked.

"Thanks, Jack. Yes I would. But first let's ring Mrs. Hopkins's bell. It doesn't sound like anyone will be home, but I'd like to try."

There was a light on in Mrs. Hopkins's kitchen. No one answered the back door.

"Let's check and see if the car is in the garage," Barnes said as the wind and rain continued.

The garage was a separate building at the end of the road. The door was locked, but through the window they could see a blue sedan.

Barnes sighed. "She obviously didn't drive away."

As the group hurried over to the Reilly home, Regan was doing her best to comfort Skip.

"What makes it even worse," he said, "is having those two busybodies in the middle of all this."

You're certainly right about that, Regan thought as they reached the front porch of the Reilly home.

6

Inside the Reillys' home, Ginny and Fran were on overdrive. They had watched intently from the windows as Jack, Regan, Skip, and the police officers came up from the beach and walked around the outside of Mrs. Hopkins's house. Ginny had already fixed another pot of coffee and Fran had redialed the window company numerous times. When the front door opened they ran to the living room, breathless with anticipation.

Regan thought the two sisters' faces resembled big question marks. Wait till they hear the news, she thought.

"Where is Mrs. Hopkins's body?" Fran asked, getting right to the point. Her eyes were blinking furiously. "Was she still alive?"

Skip grunted, peeling off his wet jacket as he walked past her. He threw it over the back of a kitchen chair, on his way to the den. He collapsed into one of the couches and put his head in his hands.

Ginny looked back and forth at Regan and Jack. "Tell us," she implored. "What happened down on the beach?"

Jack cleared his throat. "It seems as if Mrs. Hopkins's body was pulled out to sea."

"What?!!" Ginny cried, placing her hand over her mouth.

"When Skip came up here to get help, the waves got much

bigger," Jack explained. "The beach was covered with water when we went down there. She was gone."

Ginny wasn't about to keep her mouth covered for long. "I hope they find her! Otherwise we might be sitting on the beach one of these days and what do you know, here comes Mrs. Hopkins."

"Let's hope that doesn't happen," Jack answered, trying to keep his voice even. "But if her body isn't found, I'm sure it will be very difficult for her family."

The policemen, Jack, and Regan took off their wet coats.

"I want to talk to Skip," Officer Barnes explained to Ginny and Fran. "My partner, Officer Malone, and I would like to talk to you two ladies as well."

Regan could tell that even though the sisters were horrified by the news, they loved the excitement.

"We'd be happy to help in any way we can," Fran said. "Ginny, let's grab these wet coats and hang them in the bathroom."

"Certainly. And I just made a fresh pot of coffee," Ginny said proudly.

Regan hurried into the bedroom, where she kicked off her wet shoes, peeled off her socks, and changed into another pair of jeans. She felt like she'd never be warm again. Jack came in and quickly changed also. The policemen at least had been wearing protective rain gear.

Back in the kitchen they found Ginny and Fran pouring coffee.

"Have a cup," Fran insisted to Regan and Jack. "You need something to warm you up. Milk and sugar are right here."

They both accepted the mugs that the sisters extended to them.

Barnes and Malone were standing by the kitchen table, mugs in hand. Barnes was finishing up a quick call to the sergeant at his station. When he hung up, he sighed. "Let's get started."

The den had couches on the two sides of the room and a love seat in between the couches that faced the water. Barnes pointed to the couch where Skip was still bent over, his head in his hands. "Ladies," he said to the Brewers, "if you don't mind sitting there."

Skip sat up. "I feel so bad," he moaned. "I shouldn't have left her there."

When they were all seated, Officer Barnes turned to Skip. "Can you tell us again what happened?"

Officer Malone started to take notes.

Skip went through the story that he'd told the others earlier. ". . . so many of these staircases to the beach get wrecked in these storms—"

"Like ours did last year," Ginny interrupted, nodding her head. "It's terrible. They're so expensive to replace."

Annoyed, Skip briefly glanced at Ginny, then continued his story, explaining every detail. ". . . when I ran over to see what I could do about the boat, I found Mrs. Hopkins facedown at the bottom of her staircase."

"What did you do?" Officer Barnes asked.

Skip took a deep breath, his face full of pain. "I grabbed her jacket and started to turn her. What I saw was awful. Her face was bloody. I didn't know what to do, so I ran for help."

"You didn't try CPR?" Fran asked, astonished.

"No!" Skip said defensively.

"Please let me do the questioning," Officer Barnes instructed.

"Sorry."

"It was so shocking," Skip said. "I thought she was probably dead. But I wanted to get help as fast as I could."

"And you're sure that it was this Mrs. Hopkins?"

Skip nodded. "Yes. It looked like her, and she was wearing

a green jacket that I'd seen her in the other day when I was here dropping off groceries. I looked out the window and saw her crossing her backyard toward the staircase."

"Can you describe her for me?"

Skip nodded again. "She was about sixty—"

"I thought she was older than that," Ginny interrupted.

Barnes cut her off with a stern look.

"She had graying hair. She was about five foot four. She looked fit. A nice-looking face, I guess," Skip continued.

"I will say she had nice eyes," Ginny added. "Big brown eyes. Of course, I only saw them once."

Barnes turned to Jack. "You and Regan were here when Skip came running up from the beach?"

"Yes," Jack answered. "He only came into the house for a minute to tell us what happened. Regan and I immediately went back down to the beach with him. The body was gone."

"I remember once we had a picnic basket on the beach when we were kids," Ginny said nervously. "My mother had made us our favorite sandwiches. A big wave struck and washed away the basket. My mother didn't have money to buy us lunch at the food stand so we starved."

Regan smiled slightly, trying to be polite.

"Ginny, be quiet," Fran said.

"Okay," Ginny said softly. "I just know it can happen so fast. The big waves come and—"

"Shush," Fran ordered.

Barnes looked at Ginny and Fran. "Ladies, I gather you didn't have much contact with Mrs. Hopkins?"

They both shook their heads. "She didn't welcome our attempts at friendship," Fran reported.

"Not at all," Ginny said.

"She was reclusive," Fran added.

Officer Barnes nodded. "Skip, what about you? Did you know her well?"

"No. I'd call over to her if I saw her in the yard when I was working outside. But she didn't say much. Sometimes I'd see her out in that rowboat."

Ginny smiled. "She loved that rowboat. I've never seen someone go out in a boat so much in the winter. She must have had ice in her veins." Ginny's face looked as if an idea just popped into her head. "Maybe she was actually planning to go out in the boat! She might have been one of those thrill seekers! You know, like those skiers who do those crazy flips while they're coming down the mountain. I can't watch that kind of thing!"

Barnes raised his eyebrows, then turned to Jack. "You mentioned your parents know the owners of the house. Can we get their number?"

"I'm sure we can. I'll check their address book in the kitchen," Jack said, getting up from his seat.

"What are you going to do now?" Ginny asked Officer Barnes.

"We'd like to take a look inside the house. Of course her family need to be notified."

"If she has family, we never saw them!" Ginny said. "Never! Not even at Christmastime. I'm telling you we never saw anyone with her. And no visitors. You'd think she'd get lonely for conversation." She turned to Skip. "The only time we saw her talking to anyone was when we were on our back porch and looked over and saw you talking to her from the Reillys' deck."

"What's that supposed to mean?" Skip asked. "I just said that I'd say hello to her if I saw her. I was trying to be neighborly. Just like I was trying to be neighborly when I saw what was happening to her boat today. I should have kept to myself and not worried about it!"

"I didn't mean anything bad," Ginny insisted.

"Skip," Regan said, "if you hadn't checked on her boat then her family might never have had any idea what happened to her."

"I suppose," Skip muttered, looking down at the floor.

Regan looked out the window at Mrs. Hopkins's house. I can't wait to see what we're going to find in there, she thought. There must have been a good reason the woman was so reclusive.

7

In Bedford, New York, Jack's parents, Eileen and Dennis Reilly, were watching the news as they worked out in the area of their spacious basement that they'd turned into a home gym. They'd raised seven children, the youngest of whom had recently graduated from college and moved to Boston.

Dennis was jogging on the treadmill and Eileen was pedaling fast on the stationary bike. Both were in generally good shape and had recently celebrated their sixtieth birthdays. That was when they made a pact to exercise together at least three times a week.

Two of the Reilly sons worked with Dennis at the family investment firm in Manhattan. Because of the flooded roads and train delays, Dennis had opted to work from home this morning. When his time was up on the treadmill, he'd shower, then get to his desk.

Images of the storm's damage up and down the East Coast filled the television screen. They were watching a car float past a grocery store when the phone rang. Dennis, the sweat pouring down his face, waved his hand. "Let the machine pick it up. We'll check the messages when we're finished."

He knew he should have saved his breath. There was no way

Eileen, with her numerous children and grandchildren, was about to let a phone call go unanswered. She couldn't help herself. It was part of being Irish. What if something happened to someone?

"You must be kidding," Eileen answered as she stopped pedaling and got up from the bicycle. "You can see for yourself what this storm is doing," she added as she hurried over to the phone on the wall. An attractive woman with light brown hair, green eyes, and a slim frame, she looked years younger than sixty. From the caller ID she could see that the call was coming from their house on Cape Cod. "Hello," she answered quickly.

"Mom, it's Jack."

"Hi, honey, is everything all right?"

"Regan and I are fine, but there's a problem with the woman who's renting the house from the Carpenters."

Eileen felt an initial sense of relief. "What is it?" she asked, expecting to hear that the problem was minor and storm related. She and Dennis had spent a weekend at the Cape in January with another couple. They knew there was a woman living at the Carpenters', but had no contact with her. They had spotted her out in her rowboat on a particularly cold Saturday afternoon when they were sitting in the den having cocktails around the fire. They'd all joked about how lazy it made them feel.

As Jack described the events of the morning, Eileen's grip tightened on the phone. "What?" she cried. "And now she's gone?"

Dennis, hearing the concern in his wife's voice, pressed the mute button on the television and stepped off the treadmill.

Eileen gasped. "Poor Skip must be so upset."

Dennis rolled his eyes. There was always something going on with that kid. "What happened?" he whispered.

"Hold on, Jack," Eileen said quickly. "The woman living in

the Carpenters' house must have fallen down the steps to the beach. Skip found her, ran for help, then her body washed away." She turned back to the phone. "Jack, the Carpenters' number in Boston is in the address book. Isn't it in a drawer there in the kitchen? . . . Well, then check the bookshelf in the den."

Dennis frowned. His mind went back to the weekend they'd been at the Cape house in January.

". . . you found it. The number should be in there. The Carpenters were so happy when this woman came along . . . Dorie called me in November and sent a new key. She said the woman wanted the locks changed, which she did, but Dorie still felt more comfortable that we had one in case of emergencies. It's in our bedroom upstairs in my night table drawer. I left it there in January . . . Please let us know what happens . . . No, we didn't have any contact with her when we were up there."

"I did," Dennis said quickly.

Eileen looked at him. "Wait a minute, Jack. Dennis, what are you talking about?"

"Remember I ran into the post office the morning we left? That woman was standing in line to mail a package. I realized that she was the woman we'd seen crossing the Carpenters' yard after she went rowing. I said hello and introduced myself. But she obviously didn't want to talk to me. That was it."

"You didn't tell me."

"When I got back in the car, you and the Bennets were in the middle of a conversation. Then I guess I forgot. It was no big deal."

"It might be," Eileen said, handing her husband the phone. "Tell Jack."

8

An answering machine picked up at the Carpenters' home outside of Boston. Jack left a message to please call him back at his parents' house on the Cape as soon as possible. When he hung up the phone, he looked at Barnes, who was now in the kitchen.

"The Carpenters aren't home. But there's a key here that Mrs. Carpenter gave my mother to use in case of emergencies. I'd call this an emergency."

"I would too," Barnes agreed.

Five minutes later Jack and Regan went back with Barnes and Malone to the Carpenters' home. Ginny and Fran had volunteered to join them, but Barnes politely nixed the suggestion. They stayed at the Reillys' with Skip, who remained on the couch, wringing his hands and looking glum.

The rain was coming down in sheets. They assumed Hopkins had come out the back door, so they wanted to go in that way, in an effort to retrace her steps. The group hurried up onto the deck and over to the door. The Carpenters' ranch-style home had been built in the 1950s on property that was now much more valuable than the house itself. If it were ever sold, Regan was sure that a wrecking ball would roll down the block within minutes. Jack's parents had had first dibs on buying it several years ago when the last owner decided to move. He offered to sell it to them for a price that in retrospect was a bargain. To their everlasting regret, they decided against it. Not long after, the price of waterfront property skyrocketed. Then their children started to marry and produce grandchildren. It would have been a perfect spot to build a guest house for their expanding family. Regan was always amused at how much Eileen reminded her of Nora when she got that wistful look and said, "If only we'd used our heads. We let it slip through our fingers . . ."

Jack was about to put the key in the door, but turned the knob first. The door was locked. Quickly he unlocked it.

They stepped into the small kitchen. The light was on. The appliances and cabinets were old, the floor a tired linoleum. It was almost like stepping back in time. The room was clean but had a worn look. The coffeemaker was on the counter, the carafe was half full. A mug, silverware, and a plate with crumbs were in the kitchen sink.

"Looks like she had breakfast," Regan said.

"Which at least would mean she wasn't out there on the beach all night," Jack said quietly.

"How well do you know that caretaker?" Barnes asked.

Jack shrugged. "My mother knows him better. She says he's a good kid trying to find his place in the world. He loves to show up at the house when my family is around and do jobs that could have gotten done when we weren't here."

"I'm glad he doesn't want to be a doctor," Barnes observed. "It sounds like it was the sight of blood that made him run away."

Regan pushed a swinging door that opened onto the dining room. Piles of cards and envelopes were lined up neatly on the table. Regan walked over and picked up one of the cards. "I'm sorry I hurt you," she read aloud. A quick look revealed that all the cards expressed the same sentiment. Oh boy, Regan thought. If she's making this many apologies, she must have had a lot of enemies.

"I'm sorry cards?" Officer Malone asked as he picked up a sheet of paper with at least fifty names scribbled on it. First names only. "This is longer than my Christmas card list."

"No wonder this woman was a recluse," Regan said. "She probably was afraid she'd do something else she'd have to apologize for."

Jack looked at her.

"I'm serious, Jack. This woman was obviously guilt ridden."

"I thought love meant never having to say you're sorry," Barnes said wryly.

"That's bad," Malone said.

"I know."

The living room was right off the dining room. Three large plastic bags were on the floor in one corner of the room. Barnes reached for one of the bags and pulled out a decorative pillow. An index card with a note "To be picked up by Adele Hopkins" was stapled to the bag. He frowned. Embroidered on the pillow was the expression GRUDGE ME, GRUDGE ME NOT. All the pillows in the bags were exactly the same.

A pile of books took up most of the coffee table: *WAS I BORN RUDE?*, *Twelve Steps to Overcoming Irritability*, and various guides on becoming a better person through diet, exercise, meditation, and travel.

"Who was this woman?" Regan asked rhetorically. "I can't wait to hear what the Carpenters know about her."

The master bedroom was neat. The contents of the closet revealed a spartan wardrobe of plain pants and sweaters and blouses in drab colors. In the bathroom her toiletries were minimal.

"She was renting this house during the off-season," Regan said. "It's almost as if she were using it as a private retreat."

"It doesn't seem like too many people would have missed her," Barnes said. "Things here are strange, but not suspicious. A woman full of guilt and anxiety fell down the steps in the middle of one of the worst storms in years. I'm sure she had enemies, but given the circumstances, this appears to be an accident. There are accidents all over the Cape. What we have to find is information that will help us get in touch with the family in case the Carpenters are on a cruise to nowhere."

"Maybe being out in that rowboat of hers was a form of penance," Malone suggested. "If she suffered it would somehow make up for what she'd done to others."

Barnes looked at his partner with a bemused expression. "My guess is she enjoyed rowing. Plain and simple."

"I can see what you're saying," Regan said to Malone.

"Thank you."

"That's good," Barnes said. "The two of you can hash it out later over coffee."

They all chuckled.

"Now, I've never met a woman who didn't have a purse," Barnes said. "If Hopkins was just going down to the beach, she probably wouldn't have brought it with her."

They walked back down the hallway and spotted Mrs. Hopkins's purse under the dining room table, but it didn't contain a wallet or keys. There was no sign of a cell phone anywhere.

Barnes cleared his throat. "If the Carpenters don't call you back soon, we can try to get in touch with the real estate agents around here and find out who handled the rental. Hopkins must have listed someone to get in touch with in case of emergency. But for now we've got to get going. My boss said we're getting a ton of calls. It's going to be one long day."

"We'll be in touch as soon as we hear something," Jack promised.

Regan looked over at the bags of pillows. The name of the store—Pillow Talk—was emblazoned in bold blue letters on each bag. Regan remembered passing the small storefront on the way in last night. It's a few towns over, she remembered. Turning to Jack, she asked, "If we don't hear back from the Carpenters soon, do you want to take a ride over to the pillow store? If Hopkins bought this many pillows about grudges, maybe the salesperson remembers her. You never know."

"Good idea," he said, then smiled. "What about our guests?"

"Skip's the only one I'm worried about. Maybe he'll want to come with us." She sighed. "I'm afraid he's never going to get over this."

Earlier that morning

9

A huge wave crashed over Adele Hopkins. She felt herself gaining consciousness as the churning water started to carry her body, like she was on a speeding train. Terrified, she opened her mouth to scream for help and nearly choked on the salt water that flooded in. What's happening? she thought, starting to flail her arms wildly. Am I dreaming? Am I going to drown? She had always loved the sea but now it was her enemy. I've got to fight, she told herself. Drawing all the strength she could, she managed to lift her head above the water. With great relief she realized that she hadn't been pulled out to sea. The tide was all the way in.

She reached down. Her hand was able to skim the sand as the water carried her down the beach. If I can just stand up, she thought. The power of the wave started to subside and she struggled to her feet. I have a chance, she realized, as she started running desperately through the water toward the rocks. She saw a staircase nearby. It didn't look familiar. She felt disoriented and had no idea how far down the beach she'd traveled. Shivering, she grabbed the banister and made her way up the steps. Her heart was pounding. At the top there was a house set farther back than most of the houses on the water, with a large back lawn, no deck. I'm going to faint, she thought, fighting a wave of dizziness as she made her way toward the house. Was that a man looking out the window?

Suddenly the door opened. She staggered toward it.

"What are you doing, woman?" a man's voice called as he came out the door and ran toward her. He put his arm around her waist and helped her to his house. "This is no day to be out on the beach."

"I know . . ." Adele started to say. "I just . . ."

"Do you want me to call an ambulance?" he asked as they stepped into his kitchen.

"No," she said. "No."

"Your face is all banged up."

"I fell," she said. "I think I broke my nose but I'm okay. I live near here. I'll just go home." She felt such a sense of relief. This man was being so kind to her. The house was so warm and cozy. There was a delicious scent of coffee in the air. Soft classical music was playing on a radio. Why had she never seen this man before? He had a thick mane of white hair, a mustache, and the kindest face. I don't deserve this, she thought.

"Is there someone there to take care of you?" he asked.

Adele almost laughed. "No," she answered. "I live alone. I rented a house up here for the winter. When I fell I must have landed on the beach and then was carried away by a wave, I guess . . ."

"You're going to get pneumonia," he said fretfully. "You shouldn't be alone. Go in the bathroom and take a hot shower. I'll get you some clothes and a bathrobe to warm you up."

Adele didn't protest. A moment later she was gazing in disbelief at her reflection in the mirror of the medicine cabinet. Her hair was plastered to her scalp. There were cuts all over her face and her nose was slightly swollen. What happened? she wondered. I was coming down the steps. How did I fall? She took off her soaking wet clothes and wrapped a towel around her taut frame. Her teeth were chattering.

The man knocked on the door. She opened it a crack. "Here," he said, handing her a sweat suit, socks, and a fluffy bathrobe. "Get in the shower. You must be chilled to the bone. There's bacitracin in the cabinet. Dab it on those cuts on your face."

As if she were in a dream, Adele did as she was told. The man could be an ax murderer, but right now she didn't care. The hot water felt so good on her achy bones. I could have died out there, she thought. I must have been knocked out when I fell. But I don't want to go to a doctor. I want to stay right here. After several minutes she turned off the water, dried off, and got dressed. Not much I can do with my hair, she thought, applying the bacitracin to her face. Finally she opened the bathroom door and went out into the cozy living room. Bookshelves lined the room and a colorful crocheted rug covered the floor.

"How about a cup of hot tea or coffee or a bowl of soup?" he asked.

"I'd love a cup of tea. By the way, my name is Adele. What's yours?"

"Floyd. Now sit on the couch by the fire. I'll get you that tea."

"Thank you," Adele said, suddenly shy. "I don't want to take up too much of your time."

"I've got nothing but time," he replied. "You're the first visitor I've had since my wife died."

"I'm so sorry. When did she die?"

"Four years ago. Those are her sweats you're wearing. They fit you perfectly."

10

———◆———

Pippy Huegel fluffed up the pillows in the window of Pillow Talk, the shop she'd recently founded with her best friend, Ellen. It was hard to believe that less than five months ago they'd been living in a tiny apartment in Boston, both working at jobs that weren't exactly making them rich but at least provided a little bit of excitement and the promise of future advancement. Within days of each other, the two childhood friends found themselves with no reason to set their alarm clocks in the morning.

The trendy new seafood restaurant where Ellen had just been hired to plan special events went bankrupt. The owner had spent millions renovating the interior of a warehouse in an out-of-the-way location, hiring an architect whose vision was to have diners feel as if they were enjoying the delights of scuba diving while remaining dry. As it turned out, not many people wanted to travel out of their way to eat mediocre food in a room with fake seaweed hanging from the ceiling and a waterfall that sent a mildewy-smelling mist into the air.

For Ellen, it was especially hard to take. Not only was she out of work but her boss had lured her from a job selling makeup at a department store, where she'd been doing well. In bad economic times, women didn't stop buying lipstick and eye shadow. If anything, they bought more. Acquiring a new shade of lipstick became a relatively inexpensive way to lift one's spirits. Ellen had gone to work at the restaurant because the owner had promised she'd be on the fast track to a big career at one of Boston's future hot spots.

"You have people skills," he'd said when he'd bought makeup at her counter for his mother, who he said wasn't feeling well and couldn't get out to the store. Turns out his mother was having a grand time living in Florida and didn't need any help in the cosmetics department. The trunk of his car was filled with every brand of makeup on the market, all purchased as a way to meet pretty girls and get them to go out with him. But when he met Ellen, he was looking for a hostess for the restaurant who would also work with clients planning private parties. Ellen was funny, feisty, and very attractive, with long highlighted hair, big brown eyes, and a great sense of style. He marveled at her sales pitch. She had easily convinced him to buy three hundred dollars' worth of makeup that no one would ever use. He decided then and there that she'd be perfect for his venture.

Before Ellen figured out that the guy was devious, she'd quit her job and become his employee. For a month she worked hard with his staff getting reading for opening night, which seemed to go well. Reviews of the food weren't great, but her boss remained positive. Two weeks later she showed up at work to find the restaurant boarded up, a bankruptcy notice nailed to the door. Ellen was devastated. Forget severance pay—he wouldn't answer her calls. Pippy did her best to console her friend every waking moment they were together. But a few nights later Pippy came home from her job, as an assistant at a public relations firm, with an expression on her face that would stop a clock.

Ellen was stretched out on their secondhand couch, which in a few short days seemed to have acquired a permanent indentation of her body. Her head was resting against a decorative pillow embroidered with HOME OF THE RICH AND FAMOUS. "What's wrong?" she asked wearily, sure that after a moment she'd be able to steer the conversation back to her sorry state.

"I was cut loose!" Pippy wailed. "I gave them three years of my life, and they had a security guard make sure I didn't take any files and then escort me to the door. What top-secret information am I going to steal? The names of their lousy accounts? You'd think they represented Lady Gaga!"

Ellen, suddenly energized, jumped up. "I'll get the wine."

They were twenty-five years old, with no jobs, no boyfriends, and no desire to go back home and live with their parents. The lease on their apartment was up for renewal. It was mid-November and the weather was cold and raw and as bleak as they felt.

"You know," Ellen said, as she opened a bottle of pinot noir, "that guy Todd really liked me. Maybe I should have given him a chance. He's got a big job, as my grandmother says."

"No way!" Pippy replied. "You fell asleep in the car when you were on your way to dinner with him. What does that tell you?"

"I was tired."

"No you weren't. You were trying to escape. He wasn't right for you. We're only twenty-five. We don't have to surrender our ideals. At least not yet."

"But what are we going to do?" Ellen asked. "Nobody is hiring."

The phone rang. Both girls were so depressed they didn't want to answer it.

"Maybe it's someone calling with good news," Pippy suggested as she picked up the cordless phone next to the coach.

"Highly doubtful," Ellen answered as she sipped her wine.

The caller was a friend who had received a decorative pillow Pippy had embroidered and sent her for her birthday. "I love it!" Donna exclaimed. "Where can I get another one?"

"Oh, Donna," Pippy said hesitantly, sounding embarrassed. "Money has been tight. My grandmother recently taught me to embroider so I've made a few of these pillows for fun."

"You made it!" Donna cried. "That's fantastic. Can I pay you to make a pillow for my cousin who's getting married? I know she'd just love one with the names Suzy and Hank and the date of the wedding. I also could use one for a friend who just broke up with her boyfriend. You could embroider something funny about the search for Mr. Right. I'm telling you, these make great presents."

When Pippy hung up the phone, she turned to Ellen, who was staring at the television. "Remember that lemonade stand we had when we were kids?"

"How could I forget? That crabby old woman down the block called the cops because we didn't have a permit. Who does that to ten-year-olds?"

"Luckily the cops liked our lemonade, and we stayed in business. We made a decent amount of money until we got bored and closed up shop."

Ellen eyed her best friend warily. "Pippy, why are you bringing this up now?"

"When life gives you lemons . . ."

Ellen waved her hand. "I'm not setting up another lemonade stand. We're a little old for that."

"I'm not thinking lemonade. I'm thinking pillows!"

"Pillows?"

Pippy pointed to the RICH AND FAMOUS pillow where Ellen had rested her head all afternoon. "Donna loves the pillow I made for her. She thinks pillows like that make great presents and just ordered two for gifts. Let's start a business."

"I don't know how to thread a needle."

"I'll teach you. My grandmother will help us fill orders."

"Fill orders? What are you talking about?"

"We've got to do something. People need cheering up. Our pillows can be funny. You walk into a room and a pillow with a funny saying makes you smile. The pillow is talking to you like an old friend." She paused then cried out, "I know! We'll set up a store that sells pillows and call it Pillow Talk! We'll also sell cards and whatever else we can think of that will make people happy. We know *you* can sell anything . . ."

"Which led to my unemployed status."

"Ellen, you just said there are no jobs out there. We have to try something. Selling objects that make people happy is what the world needs right now."

"A need for pillows?"

"Yes. We'll embroider whatever sayings people want on them."

"Where are we going to set up shop? Out front like our lemonade stand?"

Pippy paused. "Cape Cod."

"What? In the middle of winter?"

"We have to vacate this apartment soon anyway. I'm just so glad we never signed the lease renewal. If we get our business going soon, we'll be all ready for tourist season. What do you say, Ellen? Are you going to take a chance with me?"

Ellen looked at her lifelong buddy. "I must be out of my mind. But I wouldn't let you do it without me."

The next morning they made a road trip down to the Cape, where Pippy's cousin had bought a house that he only used in the summertime. He agreed to let them stay there rent free until June and he told them about a storefront that had been vacant for over a year. They called the owner, who showed them the building, then grudgingly gave them a deal for six months with an option to renew.

They obtained a retail license, fixed up the small space with secondhand furniture, and posted notices on public bulletin boards all over the Cape. They opened before Christmas with a limited inventory. Pippy designed a website for online orders. Then they focused on Valentine's Day, embroidering dozens of red pillows with every saying they could think of about love— good, bad, and unrequited. Ellen designed Valentine's Day cards, which they reproduced at a bargain rate. She raided her grandmother's closet, bringing back to the Cape fifty-year-old dresses, which she labeled as vintage clothing, that inspired romance. They all sold out. So did their pillows. Valentine's Day sales kept their store afloat and gave them confidence they could make real money when the tourists started arriving in May. They started sewing Cape Cod pillows decorated with sailboats and expressions like GONE FISHING and HOW'S BAYOU? Their hands were cramped from embroidering pillows every night and they were starting to feel as if they'd always have to work eighteen hours a day to keep the store going.

A week after Valentine's Day they received a call from a reporter who worked at a local newspaper on Cape Cod. She was interested in writing a story about their resourcefulness and entrepreneurial spirit and desire to make people happy. They jumped at the chance to be interviewed.

The next day, the reporter came to the shop at closing time. When the three of them sat down, she asked if they minded if she taped the conversation. Naturally, they agreed.

"Let me ask how you got started," she began with a smile. There was no way she could have guessed what would come next.

"I'll tell you how we got started," Ellen said with enthusiasm, then recounted in great detail the story of her lying, conniving boss who had practically ruined her life. "Can you imagine how I felt when I saw that bankruptcy notice on the restaurant door? The man was a horror!" Ellen declared, barely pausing for breath. "If it weren't for him I wouldn't be doing this now, but still—"

"You know, we used to have a lemonade stand," Pippy interrupted.

Ellen looked at her. "Forget the lemonade stand! Tell her about what your boss did to you!" she exclaimed, then turned to the reporter. "Pippy's too polite, so I'll tell you. Her company had a security guard show her the door when she was fired after three years of devotion and hard work. It was atrocious. Now tell me, does my five-foot-two-inch friend here look dangerous to you?"

"What would you like to see happen to these people?" the reporter asked mildly.

"I wish my old boss the worst of everything," Ellen answered quickly. "You name it. For one thing, I hope that makeup melts all over the trunk of his car."

When the reporter left, Pippy, knowing the value of public relations, was terrified of how they'd be portrayed in the article. She reminded Ellen that they were supposed to be in the business of making people feel good and promoting positive thinking. "We don't want potential customers to think that we're bitter."

"I was only answering her question," Ellen insisted.

Pippy needn't have worried. When the article was published, headlined "From Lemonade to Pillows" and quoting Ellen word for word, it struck a chord. More and more people started coming into the shop, many of them anxious to share their tales about how others had done them wrong. The article was then picked up by news outlets on the internet. Suddenly the store's website was inundated with e-mails from people who had horrible stories about former bosses, teachers, coaches, anyone in a position of authority who used it as an excuse to be mean and nasty. Orders for pillows came streaming in via e-mail, the phone, and visitors to the store.

They started making pillows that said YOU'RE NOBODY TILL SOMEBODY FIRES YOU. It was their best seller. They had to hire locals to embroider so they could keep up with the orders, which made them happy. They were providing work for people, many who really needed it. Ellen formed a social group that met once a week for drinks and fun and therapeutic storytelling. She posted news of the meetings on the Pillow Talk website. Requests for interviews were pouring in. They had been discovered.

Their success was so sudden and overwhelming, it was a challenge to adjust to the rapid growth of their business and keep some sort of balance in their lives. But it was better than being unemployed.

As Pippy finished plumping the pillows, Ellen came from the back with two mugs of fresh coffee. "With this weather I don't think we'll have too many people wandering in today. At least we can get other work done around here," she said as she flipped on the radio.

"Late-breaking news," the anchor began. "This storm has caused a lot of destruction on the Cape. Just in is a report of a woman whose body is believed to have been swept out to sea. Her name is Adele Hopkins and—"

Ellen and Pippy stared at each other.

"I can't believe it!" Pippy said. "Remember when—"

Ellen waved her hand frantically. "Wait! I have to tell you

something. Last night after you had fallen asleep I was doing work on the computer. Our website received an anonymous e-mail about a horrible rowing coach named Adele Hopkins. We get people venting about others who've been mean to them, but this one was really bad. It gave me the creeps. I couldn't help but wonder if she was talking about our Adele Hopkins."

"Why didn't you tell me?" Pippy asked excitedly.

"You were asleep!"

"Show it to me now!" Pippy yelped as they both ran to the back office.

11

———◆———

Adele couldn't believe how good it felt to be with a man who wanted to take care of her. She'd deliberately isolated herself these last six months, needing time to be alone after her divorce. All the things her husband had said to her, about how none of his friends or family could ever stand her, had been so cruel. "So why did you stay in the marriage for ten years?" she'd demanded. "It's not as if we had children."

"I must have been insane," he'd replied.

"Is there someone else?" she'd asked.

"I wish!"

She'd fled to the Cape, where she knew you could keep to yourself without people thinking you're strange. Not that it was easy. Those two sisters who lived on the block would drive anyone crazy. Adele didn't want to spend two minutes with them. All she wanted to do was spend her days regaining a sense of self and figure out how to make amends with the people she'd hurt.

"Here you go," Floyd said, his fingers grazing hers as he extended a mug of tea. She was curled up on the couch, enjoying the fire, experiencing a feeling of peace that had eluded her for what seemed like forever.

"Thank you," she said, curling her hands around the cup, relishing its warmth.

Floyd sat down in the rocking chair nearby. He was so sweet and caring, but at the same time had a powerful presence that was exciting. "Feeling better?" he asked kindly.

"Much. Although I am a bit woozy."

He stared at her. "I'm not surprised. You could have drowned," he said. "Drowned!"

Adele blinked. "I know. I don't think it's hit me yet."

Floyd nodded. "Tell me about yourself."

"I'd rather hear about you," Adele said flirtatiously. "I've been living here alone for several months and I'm sick of myself."

His eyes crinkling, Floyd laughed. "Don't say that. You're a charming woman. I can tell."

"Tell me about you," she said, sipping the tea. "You must miss your wife."

"My wife?"

"Yes, when you mentioned her before I could just tell that you were close."

"Of course. You had me distracted."

Adele smiled. She was starting to feel a little uneasy. "What was she like?"

"She was a horrible woman." His eyes darkened and his voice took on an eerie tone. "A creature from the depths."

A pit developed in Adele's stomach, which she tried to ignore. "I didn't get that impression from you."

Floyd didn't answer. A shadow passed over his face. Suddenly he stood. "Friends, Romans, countrymen, lend me your ears," he boomed. "Have you ever heard that before?"

"As a matter of fact I have," Adele said as she struggled to her feet. No wonder I opted for isolation, she thought. Most people are nuts. I've got to get out of here.

"Why are you getting up? Don't you want to hear me recite the whole speech?" he asked angrily.

"Another time. I'd better get home."

"Why?"

"I think I left something on the stove."

He came toward her, his arms outstretched.

Adele tried to run.

"You're not leaving me!" he cried, grabbing her around the waist. He lifted her, carried her across the room, then dragged her down the basement steps. She tried to break away but it was useless. He was so strong. "I can't believe you wouldn't listen to me recite my lines!" he whined.

"I will. Please. Just let me go. I'll listen to the whole speech. Every last word."

"Too late now." He threw her down on a chair, grabbed a coil of rope that was hanging on the wall, and tied her up. In the corner was a radio, which he turned on, adjusting the volume until it was blaring. "There," he said. "No one will hear you if you scream for help. I'll see you later."

"Where are you going?" Adele asked desperately.

"Rehearsal. At least people there want to hear me perform."

12

When Regan and Jack went back to the Reillys', there were no messages on the answering machine, and they were amazed to find the house empty. But any fleeting fantasy that perhaps their visitors had found other lodging was dashed when they read the note that Fran and Ginny had left on the kitchen table.

Dear Regan and Jack,

    Skip is on such a guilt trip about not picking Mrs. Hopkins up and possibly saving her life (if she wasn't already dead that is), that he actually offered to board up our front window. We couldn't believe it—because we know he can't stand us. We are going to the store with him so we can pay by credit card and get our miles. After expressing our gratitude we asked if we could wait until you got back as we were dying to hear about what you discovered in the Carpenters' home. Apparently Skip's desire to ease his conscience only goes so far. He said now or never. The man is a quivering wreck. Since we couldn't reach anyone at the window place we figured we better take him up on his offer before our house is ruined. So we're off to the lumber store. See you soon, we hope. XO Fran and Ginny. P.S. Any thoughts about dinner? Skip will be joining us. We told him it's no time for him to be alone and that he should spend the night. We'll cook.

Regan and Jack looked at each other.

"I feel so sorry for him." Regan pulled a chair out and sat at the kitchen table. "The house is so peaceful. . . . This is the first minute we've been alone since you left to go to the market."

"It's hard to believe that was just a few hours ago."

"There's something that happened while you were gone that I haven't had a chance to tell you. When I opened the curtains in the bedroom this morning, Skip was right there outside the window. He jumped back and claimed he was checking for leaks. I was so startled. That's why when I heard you come in I went charging down the hall."

Jack's eyes twinkled. "It wasn't because you missed me so much? Regan, you're breaking my heart."

"Very funny. I'm telling you, Jack, even though the window was shut and the wind was howling, it was creepy."

"I'm sure it was."

"Then to have those two blabbermouths making fun of me. I'm sure they'll never stop telling that story."

Jack's face lit up. "I think I'm going to like having everyone on Cape Cod think that you come racing to greet me every time I walk through the door. It's good for my image." He leaned down and put his arms around her, leaning his head on her shoulder.

Regan smiled. "You have no problem with your image," she said, tousling his hair. "But this show of affection makes me nervous."

"Why?"

"I'm certain those two are going to magically reappear."

"We wanted to get going anyway."

Regan sighed. "Seeing all those apology cards was really sad. Adele Hopkins was trying to make amends, and then she dies like that, when she might have been saved? I am so curious to find out who she was."

"I am too. Let's hope the Carpenters call back soon. Listen, for all we know Hopkins could have been a career criminal who saw the light and came up here to repent. She might be sending cards to people she cheated in some way or it could date back to a time she stole from a friend's piggybank."

"The poor woman is dead, Jack."

"I know. But I doubt she won any popularity contests. What we found over there raises a lot of questions. And," he added, dramatically pointing his finger, "she was unfriendly to my father."

"Not good!" Regan said with a smile. "Jack, I was thinking . . . If Hopkins was trying to stay undercover and guard her privacy, for whatever reason, it must have been positively galling for her when she realized she'd rented down the block from Fran and Ginny."

"Can you imagine?" Jack said with a slight laugh. "Every time she got in her car she had to pass their house. She had to pretend not to notice when they tried to flag her down."

Regan looked at the clock on the wall. "Hopefully the Carpenters aren't out of town. With any luck, they'll be able to answer all our questions in two minutes."

"If that's the case, then let's leave tomorrow," Jack said.

Regan shook her head. "We can't do that."

"Why not?"

"Because of Skip. I'd feel terrible walking out on him now. Besides, I just have the feeling there's not going to be a simple explanation about anything having to do with Hopkins." She stood. "Let's run over to the pillow store. A good customer like Hopkins should be hard to forget."

"I also wouldn't mind getting some breakfast," Jack said. "Neither one of us has eaten anything this morning."

"That's because you gave Ginny my blueberry muffin."

"You should be happy that she enjoyed every last bite," Jack said as he reached for the phone. "I'll call the Carpenters' house and leave my cell phone number on their machine. I left them the house number before and then their message machine cut me off."

Regan pinched his cheek. "It didn't hurt your feelings, I hope."

"No. But I think I deserve one of those apology cards."

"You deserve a pillow!" Regan turned and headed out of the kitchen. "I'll get my coat and my watch and finish getting ready. I feel like I was half dressed when this day started going downhill fast."

Jack looked again in the address book and dialed the Carpenters' home. To his surprise, a breathless Dorie Carpenter answered the phone. "Whoever you are, hold on a second," she said quickly, then dropped the phone. Jack could picture the petite bouncy woman, late forties, with short blond hair and a seemingly perpetual tan. Having grown up in Boston, she had been coming down to the Cape all her life. An outdoorsy type, she loved tennis, golf, and swimming. From the time Dorie was married, she and her husband, Dan, had always rented a cottage for two weeks in the summer.

Several years ago they'd had the good fortune to hear from a friend about a man who was about to put his house on the market and was most anxious for it to sell quickly. His asking price was low because he didn't want the process to drag on, with people traipsing in and out of his home, looking through his closets and complaining about what they didn't like. He'd make a healthy profit no matter what, because he'd lived there for so many years and the house had gone up significantly in value.

Dorie, being Dorie, didn't waste a second. She got the address of the house, dragged Dan off the golf course, drove over, and rang the bell. The owner admired Dorie's pluck. Even though it stretched their budget to the limit, Dorie and Dan—especially Dorie—knew they'd be crazy to pass up the chance to own waterfront property at such a reasonable price. They'd never get an opportunity like this again. They took the plunge, making the deal that afternoon. To Jack's mother's credit, she was able to become friends with them even though she'd never get over letting that house slip through her fingers.

"I'm back," Dorie bubbled. "Hello."

"Hello," Jack responded. "This is Jack Reilly. Is that you, Dorie?"

"Yes! Hi there! I just got home from the grocery store," she said quickly, catching her breath, "and the front door blew open after I closed it. This rain is terrible. How are you?" she asked, her nerves quickening. She knew he wouldn't be calling to just chat.

"I'm okay," Jack answered. "Regan and I came up to the Cape for the weekened to celebrate our anniversary—"

"What a weekend to be at the Cape!" Dorie blurted.

That's the understatement of the year, Jack thought. "Yes, this weather is something. Dorie, I'm afraid I have some bad news about the woman who's been renting your house."

Dorie's heart sank. "What?" she asked as her yellow slicker dripped water on her kitchen floor.

"This morning our caretaker Skip went down our staircase to the beach to see if there was any damage from the storm," he began, then filled her in on the demise of her tenant.

"Oh, no!" Dorie cried. "Mrs. Hopkins floated away! Why did he leave her there? If he wasn't sure she was dead he should have—"

Jack winced. Poor Skip was going to be dealing with those questions forever. "I can assure you he's very upset," Jack said. "He obviously wishes he hadn't left her there. But he felt fairly certain that she was already dead."

"Fairly certain? She wasn't a big woman, Jack! If he had at least tried to move her—"

"Dorie," Jack interrupted. "I think he was in shock. He said that her face was bloody."

"I'm sorry. I just feel terrible. If we hadn't rented the house to her, this wouldn't have happened."

"It's not your fault," Jack assured her. "She must have slipped and fallen down the stairs. We're guessing that she was checking to make sure her rowboat was secure."

"She had a rowboat?"

"Yes."

"That's news to me."

"I saw it this morning. Apparently she was frequently on the water, even when it was freezing outside. She kept the boat tied at the bottom of your staircase." Jack then explained about going into her house with Regan and the police.

"My goodness, why was she sending out all those apology cards? She seemed like a nice, quiet, private woman. I can't imagine why she felt the need to apologize to so many people. What could she have done that was so bad?"

Oh, great, Jack thought. Dorie is supposed to be the one giving the answers, not asking the questions. "We were wondering the same thing. It could just be imagined offenses that kept her awake at night. There were also several self-help books lying around."

"Ah," Dorie said, her eyes welling with tears. "She was trying to become a better person. What kind of self-help? Do you remember any of the titles?"

"One of them was something like *WAS I BORN RUDE?*"

Dorie gasped. "I didn't find her rude at all. You see? She was probably overly critical of herself and didn't need to apologize to anyone."

"Hard to say at this point," Jack commented. "Right now we need to notify her next-of-kin. Did she put names and numbers of people to notify in case of emergency on her rental application?"

"Rental application?" Dorie asked.

"Yes. Didn't she fill out paperwork with the real estate agent?"

There was a moment of silence.

"Dorie?"

"We didn't use a real estate agent."

"Then how did you meet her?"

"This isn't going to sound good."

"Try me," Jack said, trying to lighten the tone.

"Dan and I went down to the Cape for a weekend in November. On Sunday morning we had breakfast at Fern's coffee shop. We were talking about money. The kids are both in college now and there are so many expenses. Dan said that we should probably rent out the house for at least a month during the summer. I almost choked. With our jobs we're able to go down for long weekends in June and July and then take our vacation in August. I look forward to it all year. I suggested to Dan that we register the house with a real estate agent after breakfast and try to rent it out until Memorial Day."

"What did Dan say?"

"He told me I was crazy. He said that in this economy people have a hard enough time renting their houses out in the summer. Who would we possibly get to rent our house in the winter? Well, guess what, Jack? Turns out she was sitting at the next table."

"You're kidding."

"I kid you not. It was an unbelievable stroke of luck. At least I thought so at the time. This woman Adele Hopkins overheard us. She came over, introduced herself, and said she'd just arrived on the Cape. She'd recently gotten divorced and was looking to rent a house for several months. She was a sweet woman with such sadness in her eyes. You can just imagine what happened next. Dan didn't even finish his pancakes—and the man never leaves food on his plate. We paid the bill as fast as possible and she followed us home. We couldn't believe what she offered us to stay there until May. As you know, our house is not a candidate for *Architectural Digest*. It's got a great view, but the interior has never been updated since it was built. When we have extra money, which will probably be never, we'll do it. But that doesn't matter. We have always felt incredibly blessed to have found a waterfront place at the Cape for such a steal, and to think it's worth ten times more than that now . . ."

If my mother hears that story from you one more time, Jack thought, she might resort to violence.

". . . so just like when we bought the house, we made the deal lickety-split. The next morning Mrs. Hopkins had twenty-five thousand dollars wired into our account. We were delirious. The holidays were coming and it relieved some of the pressure from all the bills that pile up. She drove over to our house and we gave her the new keys. The only thing she'd wanted was to have the locks changed, which I don't blame her for. The locksmith was there first thing in the morning."

Somehow Jack knew the answer to his next question before asking it. "Did you check her references?"

"Who wants to look for trouble when someone is handing you that kind of money?"

"I understand."

"You do?"

"Not really. But let me ask you this. Did you even ask her for references?"

"It would have been so awkward. The whole situation just felt so right, like when we bought the house. The owner had a good feeling about us when we showed up unexpectedly on his doorstep. That's how we felt about Adele Hopkins. She just appeared in our lives and we trusted her. By the way, Jack, she's not on trial, she's dead. She didn't do anything wrong. And another thing. I find it hard to believe that she fell down the steps."

"Why?"

"When we showed her around, which didn't take long because she obviously wasn't fussy, she said she was looking forward to spending time alone because her divorce had been so bitter. To live on the water would be so soothing. I asked if she had children and she said no. When we walked down the steps to the beach she had a firm grip on the railing and was very careful. She said she'd gone tumbling down a flight of steps once and was never going to let that happen again. Just the way she said it. I don't know. Maybe her ex-husband got sick of paying alimony and decided to track her down and push her down the steps again!"

"Dorie, you're jumping to wild conclusions. There is no reason to believe that something like that happened. The weather is terrible and those stairs are slippery. She shouldn't have been outside. Like I said before, we need to contact her family. Even if you didn't ask for references, surely she must have given you the name of someone to contact in case of emergency."

Again there was silence.

"Dorie?" Jack asked.

"When we gave her the keys, I asked her about who we should call if we needed to get in touch with someone on her behalf. I tried to sound delicate. But she knew exactly what I meant and joked that she didn't plan to get sick or die. She then said her best friend was moving and getting a new home number and cell phone number and she'd give them to me as soon as she had them. I called her every month to make sure that everything was okay. The first time I called I asked her for her friend's number and she said she was late for an appointment and didn't have the numbers in front of her. She wasn't much for chatting. So I didn't bother her about it again. She gave us no trouble . . ."

"So you're saying you have no contact information."

"I guess so."

"Did she use your phone? Were there any numbers on your bill?"

"No. She didn't make any calls and only answered when she could tell from the caller ID that it was me calling."

"We found no ID in the house, but her car is in the garage,

which is locked. If I can get in there and see the license plate, my office can trace it," Jack explained.

Dorie took a deep breath. "We have a key. Dan and I are coming down," she said with determination. "As soon as he gets back from the gym."

"Be careful. The driving isn't going to be easy."

"I don't care. Adele Hopkins was our tenant. She paid us fair and square and now she's dead. We have to find out who this woman was. Jack, can we pay you and Regan?"

"You don't have to pay us. We want to help. Actually, Regan and I were just heading over to the shop where she bought all the pillows to see if anyone there knows anything about her."

"Oh, great. And don't forget, we met her at Fern's. She said the breakfast had been delicious. Maybe she went back. Fern knows everything that's going on around town. Which reminds me of Fran and Ginnie. If you talk to them—"

"Believe me, we have. A branch crashed through their front window this morning. They came over and plan to stay indefinitely."

"You poor dears."

"That's for sure."

"That's another thing. With those two living on the block, I knew I'd hear from them if Mrs. Hopkins was doing anything crazy. They're like our own neighborhood watch."

"That they are," Jack agreed.

"Jack, thank you for all your help. We're so lucky to have you and Regan down there. I don't know what we'd do without you. We'll see you as soon as we can."

Jack hung up the phone. By now, Regan was standing next to him. He'd been holding the phone out so she could hear the conversation.

"You were right, Regan. There's no simple explanation for who that woman was."

Regan smiled. "Yes, but I didn't expect there'd be *no* explanation. Let's go. Something tells me that anyone on the Cape who had fleeting contact with Adele Hopkins knows more about her than Dorie."

13

―――――◆―――――

Aren't we lucky to have found such a wonderful spot for breakfast?" Devon asked as he and five of his six actors piled into a minibus outside Fern's. "We all need to start the day with a hearty, healthy breakfast. From this moment on we're going to need every ounce of energy!"

"Um-hmm," the others grumbled. Being theater people, they didn't relish the morning.

Devon turned on the ignition and pulled out of Fern's parking lot onto a narrow, slick road. A mile later, as their home away from home—a magnificent white mansion perched on a slope overlooking the sea—came into view, Devon outstretched his right arm. "How can we be this lucky?" he asked dramatically. "Before long we'll be entertaining theatergoers on that sprawling lawn. They'll be sitting in seats under an open-air tent, sniffing the sea air . . ."

"In weather like this, they're especially going to love it," one of his actors remarked.

"Oh, Brandon"—Devon chuckled—"we'll pull down the flaps. Our audiences will be so transfixed, they won't care where they are."

"The lodging is what I like," Martha commented. "I've performed in places where they put us up in school dormitories that should have been shut down by the board of health."

"Haven't we all?" Annie, the rep's ingenue, agreed. She winked conspiratorially at Martha. "Living in that mansion is great, but I'd really like my own house."

"Me, too!" Martha exclaimed.

Devon gasped. He knew that his cast loved to tease him. Naturally he loved the attention.

The traveling theater company was his baby. Over the years he'd written plays that had been produced but never made a lasting impression. This last year, though, he'd written a play that had been well received at readings for investors in New York City. Devon glowingly described his creation as a comedy about a typical dysfunctional family weekend in the country. His goal, of course, was to have the play produced on Broadway. But first it would have to be tested on out-of-town audiences. No doubt the script would have to be tweaked here and there along the way.

Devon raised enough money from investors to cover the cost of producing his play in three locations over the summer. First stop Cape Cod, then the Berkshires, and finally the Hamptons. In each place Devon had managed to find a welcoming spot to pitch his tent. He'd auditioned hundreds of actors, finally coming up with a cast that he felt was perfect to fill the roles he created—a mother and father in their mid-forties; their son and daughter, both in their early twenties; the daughter's troublesome boyfriend; and the pivotal role of the nutty grandpa who comes to visit.

He was wild with anticipation to get started with the rehearsals. Tomorrow night's cocktail party would be fun, but after that they'd get down to business, doing what they all loved best. The rehearsal process was a period of discovery that was most exciting. He couldn't wait to guide the actors, desperately hoping that they'd mine every ounce of gold out of every brilliant line of his play.

Only one thing made him nervous—the thought of directing Floyd Wellington, the actor who was playing Grandpa. Floyd was a star of the theater world who had strong opinions about every aspect of every production he'd ever been a part of.

It had been a coup to get him to do one of the readings in New York. All the comments from investors were that Floyd Wellington was born to play the part. Many of them would invest only if he *did* play the part. Wellington's range as an actor was unmatched. Onstage he was always captivating, unpredictable, mercurial, sometimes crazy as a loon, and charming when need be. Unfortunately, he was the same way offstage. The guy couldn't gas up his car without making it some kind of performance. He had been in one hit movie and then declared the whole experience bored him. He'd never waste his time again. In the years that followed he received numerous film offers, but it didn't matter. He'd made up his mind. If anything, he saw his life as a movie.

Floyd agreed to join the Traveling Thespians on their summer tour, but he made it clear he had no desire to live in a group situation, mansion or no mansion.

"I would never expect you to," Devon had fawned.

For their Cape Cod stay, Devon had rented a lovely home on the water where Floyd would live, alone.

Devon knew that the success of the play depended on Floyd. He was certainly the draw for the cocktail party. People who'd seen him in his one movie forty years ago and those who'd seen him on Broadway were anxious to make his acquaintance.

Pulling the Thespians' minibus down the long driveway, Devon was surprised to see Floyd's car already there. He's not due for another half hour, Devon thought. It's not like him to be early.

Inside the house he found Floyd glued to the television in the spacious kitchen. Like most everyone on the Cape, he was watching storm coverage.

"Good morning, Floyd," Devon said cheerily. "Didn't expect to see you here this soon."

Floyd smiled. "I can't wait to get started, Devon. This role is something I can sink my teeth into." His eyes blazed as a growling noise emanated from his throat.

Whew, Devon thought. He's in a good mood. "Would you like a cup of coffee?"

"No."

Across the television screen the words BREAKING NEWS appeared in bold red lettering. "We have a very sad story to report," the male anchor announced. "A woman renting a home on Pond Road in Chatwich has presumably been swept out to sea. We are warning everyone to please stay off the beaches. The currents are—"

"What a shame," Floyd said as he turned to Devon, his face bereft. "A story like that fills me with a sadness that I draw on when I act."

"How interesting," Devon said, shaking his head meaningfully. "Even though you didn't know her you'll be able to use her loss in a performance."

Floyd nodded solemnly. "I can't wait to find out more about her. It will make me even sadder and enrich me." A moment later he chuckled. "Hey, Devon, hopefully she wasn't someone who was going to write a big check at our cocktail party tomorrow night. After all, timing is everything!" His booming laugh filled the room.

This play better make it to Broadway, Devon thought as he pretended to find the joke amusing. I was warned about this guy. Maybe I should have listened.

But I need him.

14

When Regan and Jack turned into the gravel parking lot of Pillow Talk, a cute little shop set back from the road and surrounded by trees, Jack shook his head. "I can't believe that this is where the shop is."

"Why?" Regan asked as Jack steered the car into a parking spot near the entrance. "It seems like a perfect location for a store like this. And the building is so charming—the quintessential Cape Cod cottage." She paused. "What's wrong with it?"

Jack turned off the car. "It *is* a perfect location. But for shopkeepers there have been problems."

"What kind of problems?"

"This place was a tailor shop for more than forty years. The owner died and the family sold the property about five years ago. It seems that every year since, there has been a new tenant. You probably didn't notice, but last summer it was vacant."

"Why so many changeovers?"

"The owner made life difficult for his tenants. When it was an ice cream store he'd come in and sit there for hours, making suggestions about how they could drum up business, then ask for a free sundae. When it was a dress shop he'd stop by and plop down in the chair reserved for weary husbands. If a woman asked him what he thought of the outfit they were trying on, he'd just shake his head and give it the thumbs-down. No one ever wanted to renew their lease. I guess that's why it was empty last year. Word gets around."

"That guy must be lonely. We should introduce him to Fran and Ginny." Regan opened the car door. "The new tenants must be optimists or from out of town."

Bells on the door tinkled as Regan and Jack walked inside the shop.

The first thing that caught Regan's eye was a pillow propped on a shelf that read YOU'RE NOBODY TILL SOMEBODY FIRES YOU. Jack saw it too.

"An interesting philosophy," he muttered.

The room itself, painted a pale yellow, was cheerful. Rows of greeting cards lined one wall. On another wall were shelves of embroidered pillows that made for interesting reading. Another one that caught Regan's eye was EX MARKS THE SPOT.

A round table with four chairs covered by a flowered tablecloth was in the corner. Hanging on the wall right by the entrance were several framed newspaper articles. Regan stepped closer to read the headline: Two Best Friends Have Been Turning Lemons into Lemonade Since They Were Ten Years Old.

A young woman came hurrying out of a back room. "Hello," she said cheerfully. "My name is Ellen. Can I help you with anything or would you just like to look around?"

Jack extended his hand. "My name is Jack Reilly and this is my wife, Regan. My parents have a home in Chatwich. We're here to see if you have any information about a woman who purchased at least a dozen pillows from this store. Her name was Adele Hopkins."

Ellen's face flushed. "Pippy," she yelled, "get out here!"

You'd think we were about to rob the place, Regan thought. But she obviously remembers Hopkins.

Pippy arrived in a flash. She was petite with curly brown hair and a sweet face that at the moment bore a worried frown. "What is it?"

"These people are asking about Adele Hopkins."

"Oh my. We heard about what happened to her on the news. We can't believe she's dead!"

"We're in shock," Ellen agreed. "I don't mean to be rude, but why are you involved?"

Jack explained what he and Regan did for a living. "But we'd want to help out anyway. My parents have a home next door to the house Mrs. Hopkins was renting. The owners of that house are friends of ours."

Pippy gestured to the table in the corner. "Please sit down. Would you like coffee?"

"No thanks," Regan and Jack both answered.

If they're asking us to sit down, they must know something, Regan thought. As they headed to the table, she said, "We realized your store must be fairly new. How long have you been here?"

In a whirl, Ellen explained their story. "After that first newspaper article appeared six weeks ago, it spread like wildfire on the internet. We have so many orders for pillows, we can hardly keep up. Our website has gone crazy. So many people have written to us with their stories of being fired, or of people who have done them wrong. Which brings us to Mrs. Hopkins."

"What about her?" Jack asked.

"Well, we first met her in January when she stopped in and asked if we carried stationery. We don't, so she starting browsing through the cards and checking out the pillows. This was before that first story about us appeared and we started making all the pillows with jokes about being fired and that kind of thing. But at that time some of our pillows had quips about ex-boyfriends and expressions about not letting the bad guys get you down."

"We started this store with the purpose of selling pillows and cards that were funny and would cheer people up," Pippy interrupted. "Our success is great but now that our website has become a place for people to vent, we're hearing from a few people who are obviously quite angry."

"I'm getting to that," Ellen insisted. "So Mrs. Hopkins was here and looking at the pillows when she turned to me and said that maybe some of these bad guys who'd let people down feel sorry about what they had done but didn't know how to express themselves. I told her they could send an apology card, and that we had just received our first shipment. It was Pippy's suggestion that we order them. Mrs. Hopkins asked if she could see them. I brought a few out and she bought four boxes! She could tell I was surprised, then mumbled something about knowing someone who could really use them."

"It's the old 'I'm buying this for my friend,'" Pippy interjected. "But it made us wonder. Then she asked about custom-made pillows. We said we could embroider anything she wanted. She ordered a dozen pillows, all alike—'GRUDGE ME, GRUDGE ME NOT'"—and asked if she could pick up one as soon as possible. At that time Ellen and I were making all the pillows ourselves. I said sure, I'll make it tonight. She picked it up the next day. Then she came by over a month later to pick up the rest of them, the day the first newspaper reporter came in to interview us. Mrs. Hopkins was walking out as the reporter was walking in. I think it made her uncomfortable when the reporter asked her what her pillows said. She just sailed past the reporter and said, "Nothing special."

Ellen nodded. "The reporter asked us again after Mrs. Hopkins was gone, but we didn't tell her because it wouldn't have been right. She might have tried to find out Mrs. Hopkins's name, and who wants the world to know that you're asking tons of people for forgiveness?"

"I told the reporter she had selected an assortment of pillows," Pippy added earnestly.

"And that was the last time we ever saw Mrs. Hopkins," Ellen said.

This doesn't help much, Regan thought. "Did she say anything about—"

"Wait. I'm not finished," Ellen blurted.

"Okay," Regan said, trying to smile. This woman should meet Ginny.

"That afternoon we received one of the pillows we had made for her in the mail. It obviously must have been that first one she picked up. It was slashed to ribbons."

Regan and Jack both leaned forward.

"Was there a return address?" Regan asked.

"Nope. Nothing. The postmark was from Long Branch, a town south of Boston."

"Hopkins mustn't have put a return address on the package when she sent it out," Jack said. "How did whoever received it know where to send it back?"

"All of our pillows have a little tag sewn in the corner with our name and address," Pippy answered. "I used to work in PR. You can't be shy about promoting your product."

Ellen pushed her hair behind her ear. "We couldn't get in touch with Mrs. Hopkins because we didn't have any information about how to reach her. She paid cash and didn't want to be on our mailing list. When she walked out that day the newspaper reporter was here, that was it. We felt terrible but in a way it was a relief. Can you imagine handing the pillow back to her all slashed to ribbons?"

"Did you keep it?" Regan asked.

"Of course. It's in the back."

"If you don't mind," Jack said, "I'd like to take it with us."

"It's all yours," Pippy said quickly. "There's one more thing."

"What?" Jack asked.

"Last night we received one of those nasty e-mails I told you about. The subject line was 'Adele Hopkins—the rowing coach from hell.' "

"Really?" Regan said.

"Yes. Ellen read it last night. It was from someone who said that her rowing coach, Adele Hopkins, had been the meanest, most horrible woman she'd ever met. Hopkins berated girls on the team who weren't as good as the star athletes. She made their lives miserable. This person wrote that Hopkins was a five-foot-four-inch tyrant with a pug nose that she'd love to break."

"How tall was the Hopkins you're talking about?" Regan asked delicately.

"About five-three," Ellen answered. "She had curly hair and a cute pug nose."

"You say whoever wrote this didn't sign their name?" Jack asked.

"No, they didn't," Pippy affirmed. "Ellen and I heard the news on the radio about Mrs. Hopkins and then she told me about the e-mail. When I read it for myself, I fired back a response and said, 'You might be interested to know a Mrs. Adele Hopkins who was living on Cape Cod just died in a terrible accident. Hopkins was a lovely woman. You should be ashamed of yourself.' "

Oh no, Regan thought. "Did this woman write back?"

"Not yet. I don't expect her to."

"If you don't mind, I'd like a copy of that e-mail as well as the pillow," Jack said.

"Do you think it was the same Adele Hopkins?"

"It's possible. Mrs. Hopkins had a rowboat."

Ellen and Pippy both gasped.

"If you get any more e-mails about her, will you please let us know?" Regan asked.

"But please," Jack added quickly, "don't respond until you talk to us."

"Don't worry," Pippy said. "And we'll ask everyone who comes through the door today if they know anything about her. You never know."

"That's right," Regan agreed. "You never know."

15

Adele felt terrified. Her hands were tied behind her back, her feet secured to the bottom of the uncomfortable straight-back chair. She'd tried numerous times to loosen the ropes but it was no use. A thought occurred to her that almost made her laugh. If Floyd had tied up my boat, I wouldn't have had to worry.

Who was this nut? she wondered. Was he really headed to play practice? If he is, I guess I can't blame myself for trusting him so much. He certainly was convincing in the part of the concerned neighbor, the lonely widower.

But boy, could he change fast. It was scary. I don't want to think about what he might be capable of.

Adele felt a chill go through her body. The basement was damp and gloomy and smelled of mildew. Thumping music was blaring from the radio, making her feel even more jittery and afraid.

Is he renting this house? Adele wondered. Or does he live here? I came up here so no one would find me. Right now I certainly got what I wanted, she thought bitterly. It's not as if anybody is going to look for me. No one will notice I'm not around, except maybe those two sisters. It'll probably only be when it's time for me to clear out of the Carpenters' house next month that anyone will realize something is wrong.

She closed her eyes, thinking back on the events of the morning. She'd risen early and made a pot of coffee. She had breakfast, showered, and dressed. Her computer was finally repaired, and she was going to pick it up.

Tears stung her eyes. If only I hadn't gone to check on the boat. But the wind was howling and shrieking. I was afraid it would break into pieces. Or break loose from the staircase. I ran across the lawn, grabbed the railing, went several steps down, and suddenly slipped. I remember tumbling down . . . and hitting the beach. The next thing I knew water was covering me and I was being tossed around . . .

The thumping music finally ended. Please, she thought, I'd rather hear anything than more of that music.

"Hello out there, folks," a male D.J. began. "This is Charles Bingley. I'm going to tell you about a breaking story I just picked up on Twitter."

Thank God, Adele thought.

"Ladies and gentlemen," Charles continued, "a woman who rented a house here on the Cape was washed out to sea. Her name is Adele Hopkins."

"What?" Adele cried out. "Why would they think that? And how would they know already?"

"Folks, what makes this story even more heartbreaking is that no one seems to know much about this woman. Her neighbors certainly didn't. As of now, she's a mystery."

"So what?" Adele said aloud, tears pouring down her cheeks. "That's the way I wanted it."

"The man who found her on the beach ran to get help, and she was washed away. Can you imagine the guilt? Can you just imagine it?"

"What man?" Adele screamed.

"He must feel terrible," Charles opined. "It was only yesterday I was feeling sorry for the woman who fell into a Monet painting while visiting a museum and made a six-inch gash in it. I thought the fact that the painting was now worth millions less would be hard for her to live with. But what we're talking about today is the loss of human life!"

"Another tweet, just in—she had numerous apology cards on her dining room table she obviously planned to send out. There were decorative pillows she'd bought recently that must have been intended for people who held a grudge against her. Adele Hopkins was a tormented soul. I'd like to find out why."

Adele felt as if an electric shock had gone through her body. How mortifying. I knew those apology cards were a stupid idea. And who was it who found me?

Suddenly she felt a flicker of hope. I sent out one of the pillows. Maybe they'll hear about what happened to me and let people know who I am. Then reality struck. It doesn't make a difference.

They think I'm dead.

16

Sitting in his luxury apartment in Boston, Reed Danforth's face was tense, his jaw clenched. A man in his late forties with graying hair, and a face that only from a great distance might be considered handsome, he was about to log on to Pillow Talk's website. Ever since he'd learned that his former employee was gaining notoriety after her terrible experience with him, he checked her website daily. That first newspaper article about Ellen's pillow store contained his name and the name of his failed restaurant in big bold letters. It was hard to believe that was only six weeks ago. Many people he had considered friends taunted him about supposedly buying makeup as a ruse to meet girls. He'd been about to close a few deals but investors backed off quickly when they found out what a jerk he'd been.

"Unfortunately it was better for us to cut our losses as soon as we realized the restaurant was not going to turn a profit," Reed would try to explain. "Naturally it's an upsetting situation for everyone."

"But lying about your mother being sick?" one potential investor in an apartment building restoration asked him. "That's pretty low."

His mother agreed. She called from Florida the moment she

heard about his escapades from an internet addict at her bridge club. "Reed dear," she said, "weren't you afraid you were going to jinx my health by saying I was sick? You know I have aches and pains. My sinuses are acting up, my feet hurt at the end of the day. But to say I couldn't leave the house? Is talk like that going to help me find another husband?"

"I'm sorry, Mom."

"You may as well throw all that makeup in a box and send it down here. I'll share it with my girlfriends."

"I already gave it away—" he began.

His mother hung up.

He remembered with regret the day Ellen pulled up next to him in the parking lot of the restaurant. His trunk was open and he was digging something out of the glove compartment. Before he could get out of his car, she was staring into his trunk.

"How much makeup does your mother need?" she'd teased.

"It was a good way to meet girls," he'd joked, shrugging his shoulders. "I have no luck on those dating sites."

"A way to meet girls?" Ellen asked, her face quizzical. "Really?"

Soon after, the restaurant closed, and his life went steadily down hill. It crashed when Ellen's article hit the world wide web.

I hate the internet, Reed thought, as he typed in Pillow Talk's website address. There's no such thing as privacy anymore. If I hadn't lost my job at Sweetsville, this whole thing would never have happened. I gave them the best years of my life.

Sweetsville was a national company that sold ice cream. His position as a senior executive paid well enough to cover the alimony he sent his ex-wife on the first of every month, and an upscale lifestyle for himself. Then one day he was called in by his boss and given the old heave-ho. Somehow his company would have to manage without him. "Sales of our wonderful products," his boss said sadly, "have dipped. Everyone's on a diet."

Ironically enough, like so many of the people who wrote on the message boards at Pillow Talk, Reed knew the pain of being fired.

After his long stint at Sweetsville, which he had expected would end at retirement age, he couldn't find a new job. Unwisely, he decided to open a restaurant. His older sister was rich and willing to invest, and so were many of his wealthy friends. Between his trips to the makeup counters around town, he put his plans into action. It took time but the restaurant was renovated, the fish tanks were carted in, and the staff was hired.

It was amazing how quickly everything fell apart. The reviews were bad and the restaurant was already in debt. I should have warned Ellen that we were closing, and I should have returned her phone calls, he thought for the millionth time. When it all happened my life was a seesaw. On the one hand he had investors screaming at me, and on the other he had the love and attention of a wonderful woman whom he'd met three weeks before the restaurant opened, and it wasn't even at a makeup counter. They'd literally bumped into each other on the street. Sparks flew, and they fell in love. He convinced himself that it wasn't because she was beautiful, ten years younger, and turned out to be rich.

In those first three weeks after they met, it was magical and crazy. Working to get the restaurant ready, he stole away whenever he could and raced to see her. Opening night Olivia was out of town on business, a trip she couldn't cancel. Then she had to visit her ailing father. The restaurant closed before she got back. He'd been so afraid that she'd think he was a loser. Luckily she didn't. She was sympathetic and understanding. He couldn't believe this amazing woman was in his life. Then when the news broke about what he'd done to Ellen and how he'd buy makeup to meet girls, he was sure that his relationship with Olivia would be over. To his surprise, she was even sweeter than before.

"You were buying that makeup before you met me," she said. "So I don't care. I'm just glad you didn't meet anyone you really liked while you were buying eye pencil! As for this pillow girl Ellen, you should have called her and apologized that the restaurant failed, but you were in such a terrible state. We all make mistakes." She'd stroked his hair. "We knew from the minute we met each other that this was it for life. There'd never be anyone else. Right, honey?"

"Of course." He'd smiled and kissed her, but in the back of his mind he was nervously reliving the one thing she'd never forgive him for. As the weeks went by he was grateful that Ellen had never mentioned anything about it in her interviews. Hopefully she never would.

Quickly he scanned the website. There was a notice that Ellen and Pippy were so sad that a woman who had been in their store a few times had been swept out to sea in the terrible storm.

Phew, he thought. That's the big news of the day.

Next he went to the question-and-answer section. Every day at noon either Ellen or Pippy sat at the computer for a half hour and opened their website to a live discussion. People from all over the country asked questions or made comments. The audience had grown by leaps and bounds. All thanks to me, he thought sarcastically. It was amazing how many people out there wanted to vent. Romances had even sprung from the website. People were arranging get-togethers in different cities. Why couldn't I have this kind of success with a business? he wondered.

Reed soon realized that today the discussion was a little different than usual. It wasn't only about people's negative experiences when they were fired or mistreated. Ellen wrote that she'd read an article that said apology websites were popping up on the internet. People were going online to apologize for things they'd done, some a long time ago. They were hoping that the people they'd hurt, and didn't know how to get in touch with, would read their regrets online and in their hearts forgive them. "Would any of you be willing to accept an apology like that?" Ellen asked.

The first response was "Maybe. But only if it sounded like the person really meant it."

Another thought the internet was too public a forum. "Who wants everyone to read that someone's sorry they called you ugly in the third grade?"

The next response made Reed's blood run cold. "No way! Years ago, before you could sue for these kinds of things, my married boss chased me around his desk when we were working late in his office. He tried to kiss me and I'm telling you it was absolutely disgusting. Not that I'm into looks, but this guy was a married troll. I would never ever forgive him! Ellen, did that terrible boss of yours who bought all the makeup ever do anything like that to you? You're such a pretty girl. He sounds like the type who would at least try something."

Reed froze as he waited for Ellen's response.

"Oh, he is."

"What happened?" the woman typed.

"The opening night of the restaurant he was drinking champagne and being very flirtatious. He gave me a quick kiss on the lips and said he knew I thought there was too much of an age difference between us but if there weren't he'd make me fall in love with him."

"What did you do?"

"Pretended to laugh, then disappeared into the crowd. The restaurant closed soon after. Just last week I heard he was already into a hot and heavy relationship with someone he'd recently met. She was out of town for the opening."

Reed collapsed on his sofa as the door to his apartment flew open. "Honey, I'm back!" Olivia cried. "Did you have a nice morning?"

17

When Ellen's live session on the Pillow Talk website ended, she got up from the computer and walked out to the showroom. Pippy was at the counter, ringing up a sale for an elderly woman.

"No, I never met her," the woman said as she signed a credit card receipt. "But I'll be sure to keep her in my prayers."

"Thank you. Be careful out there in this rain."

The woman waved her cane. "I've lived on the Cape all my life. This storm is bad, but I've lived through some beauties." She paused. "I was a go-go dancer, you know."

"Oh really?" Pippy said politely.

"That's right, dear. I got fired last week." Chuckling at her own joke, the octogenarian headed for the door. "'Bye now."

Pippy was laughing too. "'Bye. Please come back."

"I'll do my best."

With a smile, Ellen walked over to the counter. "I hope I'm like that when I'm her age."

"Me too," Pippy answered. "How was the web chat?"

"Fine until someone asked me a question about Danforth."

"What did they ask?"

"They wanted to know if he'd ever made a pass at me."

"Uh-oh."

"I was honest, and I kept it light, which it was. As you know, I wasn't upset until I heard he was in a relationship when he hit on me. What if I had liked him? It just proves my point that the man is a snake." She shook her head. "If I had found out about his relationship before our first newspaper interview, I definitely would have mentioned it."

"Mentioned it?" Pippy asked airily as she came from behind the counter. "You'd have done more than that."

"Maybe," Ellen agreed. She sighed. "I can't stop thinking about Mrs. Hopkins."

"Could have fooled me."

"Pippy! You know I feel terrible."

"Of course," Pippy answered softly. "Me too. Would you like a cup of coffee?"

"No, I'm all right."

Pippy walked into the back room. She started to reach for the coffeepot, then quickly turned and sat at the computer. I'm going to obsess about this all day, she thought as she pulled up the list of their received e-mails. Three seconds after the list appeared onscreen, a burst of adrenaline flowed through Pippy's body. There it was! The address of the person who'd written about Adele Hopkins. Whoever it was had responded two minutes ago!

The bells on their front door started tinkling. Oh, no! Pippy thought. I want to read this with Ellen. But there's no way I can wait until the customer leaves. Holding her breath, she pointed the cursor to the e-mail and pressed down her finger.

Pippy's first impression was one of surprise that the font was quite different than the last e-mail they'd sent.

LISTEN UP, MISS PILLOW TALK!
YOU HAVE SOME NERVE INVITING PEOPLE TO WRITE IN

AND SHARE THEIR PROBLEMS AND THEN TAKING SUCH A RIGHTEOUS TONE WITH ME. I'M SORRY TO HEAR THAT YOUR CUSTOMER ADELE HOPKINS DIED. IF SHE WAS THE ADELE HOPKINS I KNEW, THEN SHE'LL END UP IN THE RECORD BOOKS FOR LIVING TO THE RIPE OLD AGE OF AT LEAST 110. I'M 87 AND I'LL NEVER FORGET THE WAY THAT WOMAN TAUNTED AND HUMILIATED SO MANY YOUNG GIRLS, ESPECIALLY ME.

DON'T BOTHER TO RESPOND BECAUSE IF I SEE YOUR ADDRESS I'LL PRESS THE DELETE BUTTON AS FAST AS MY ARTHRITIC FINGERS WILL ALLOW.

I LOOK FORWARD TO READING ON THE INTERNET THAT YOUR BUSINESS HAS GONE DOWN THE DRAIN.

GOOD RIDDANCE.

Pippy sat there in disbelief. And I'm the one always warning Ellen about being impulsive, she thought. I should have cooled down before I sent that response this morning. If this person is for real, then the Adele Hopkins she knew must have caused her a lot of pain.

I wish I could talk to Ellen right now, Pippy thought anxiously. But customers were still in the store. She reached for the phone. One thing I can do is tell Regan and Jack Reilly.

18

Ginny and Fran rode with Skip in his aging pickup truck over to House Junction, a warehouse-size store that sold just about everything needed to maintain a home. A trip that should have taken twenty minutes stretched out to forty-five. They were diverted from flooded roads twice, then found themselves in a traffic jam caused by a multicar fender bender.

Sitting in the middle, it was an effort for Ginny not to get tossed one way against Skip, or the other against Fran, every time they hit a bump. She was wearing a seat belt but it didn't matter. The truck seemed devoid of shocks or springs.

It hadn't surprised her in the least when Fran had run out of the house ahead of her, opened the passenger door, then stepped aside, and said, "After you.' " Even though I'm sixty-three, Ginny thought, Fran is still the big sister who gets the good seat.

"This is so nice of you, Skip," Ginny had said as they started the trip. "Fran and I are very grateful."

He'd mumbled a response, then turned on the radio, immediately switching from his favorite rock station to one that played soft classical music.

"I know you did that for us," Ginny said with a laugh. "That was very thoughtful."

"Indeed it was," Fran agreed as she stared straight ahead, her right hand holding tight to a grip above the passenger door.

After a few stabs at general conversation, Ginny gave up. It was clear Skip was in no mood to talk. They bumped along, the soft classical music nearly drowned out by noisy windshield wipers. When Skip finally pulled his truck into the crowded parking lot of Home Junction, Ginny clapped her hands. "Here we are!"

"I'll drop you off at the entrance," Skip said, "then find a space. No sense you two getting wet . . ."

They all tensed at the unintended irony of the words that had just escaped his lips.

Skip hit the steering wheel with his hand. "I should have worried about Mrs. Hopkins getting wet."

Ginny reached over and put her hand on his shoulder as he drove slowly through the lot. "Oh Skip," she said softly. "You can't do this to yourself."

Skip just shook his head.

An announcer's voice suddenly came over the radio, loud and clear. "Time for our top of the hour newsbreak. We've received word of the tragic death of a woman named Adele Hopkins . . ."

In a flash, Fran reached over and snapped off the radio. "We don't need to listen to that."

"No we don't," Ginny agreed. "Skip, don't drop us off. We'll look for a space with you."

"No." Skip replied.

"We insist," Fran said firmly.

"I insist," Skip replied as he pulled to the entrance and stopped. "I know you're doing what you can to make me feel better. But nothing's going to change what happened. I'm going to have to somehow, someday, come to terms with it. I don't know how, but at this moment I just want to park the car. So please, go ahead inside. I'll be there in a few minutes."

Ginny patted his shoulder. "We'll be waiting for you."

19

Regan and Jack were welcomed heartily as they walked into Fern's diner.

"Look who's back!" Fern called out, rushing over and shaking their hands. "It's great to see you. But what are you doing on Cape Cod on a weekend like this?"

"Sunday's our first anniversary," Jack said with a grin, putting his arm around Regan. "She's still hanging in there."

Regan smiled. "We thought we'd come up for a quiet weekend, but—"

"I heard," Fern interrupted. "Come sit at my table."

In the corner, Fern's table served as her home base, a place where she ate her own meals while keeping an eye on the front door, an office where she did paperwork and met with suppliers, and—on occasions like this—a spot where she could sit and talk privately with special guests.

As they followed Fern across the bustling restaurant, Regan noticed that people were keeping an eye on the TV. Not surprisingly, a quick glance revealed that the station was covering the storm. When she and Jack were seated, a freckle-faced waitress who looked as if she couldn't be much older than twenty, offered them coffee, which they accepted.

"I'll be right back," Fern said quickly. "I have to check on one table, then I can join you." She hurried off.

"Menus?" the waitress asked.

Jack held up his hand. "I think we both know what we're having. If you don't mind, I'd love to order right away. We haven't eaten all day."

"Sure," the young girl responded, putting the menus down on the table, then pulling a pad and pencil out of her pocket. "Fire away," she said with a giggle.

After they placed their orders for breakfast food, the waitress scooped up the menus. "I'll tell the cook to make this fast!" she said, then hurried toward the kitchen.

"What a nice kid," Regan said, just as Jack's cell phone rang. He pulled it out of his pocket and looked at the caller ID.

"Must be someone from around here," he said. "Hello . . . oh, yes, Pippy."

Pippy's calling so soon? Regan thought. As she listened to Jack's half of the conversation, she was able to get the gist of what Pippy was telling him.

"Thanks for letting us know," Jack said. "We'll keep in touch." He put his phone down on the table.

"It wasn't our Adele Hopkins?" Regan asked.

"Not unless she was very well preserved," Jack answered, then gave Regan the details.

"We can still try to get in touch with the woman who sent the e-mail," Regan said. "It's probably a long shot, but maybe our Adele Hopkins is related to this other Adele Hopkins. A love for rowing could be in the genes."

"It's possible. But our Hopkins was Mrs. Hopkins. If that was her married name, then she wasn't related by blood."

"And what about us?" Regan asked.

Jack's eyes widened. "You're absolutely right, Regan Reilly Reilly."

Fern came over and plopped down into a seat. "Hello again. You must have had an exciting morning. Skip found the neighbor's body?"

Regan cringed. Poor Skip.

"Yes," Jack answered, then related to Fern just what happened.

Fern pointed back to the TV. "About twenty minutes ago they did a report from the Carpenters' backyard."

"Already?" Regan asked. "What did they say?"

"Nothing you don't know, I'm sure. The reporter was quite dramatic. He was standing by the staircase down to the beach and began the story with something like, 'Adele Hopkins couldn't possibly have known that when she started down these very steps this morning, her life was about to come to an end.' " Fern waved her hand. "Give me a break."

"I hope he's not there when we get back," Jack said.

"Don't count on it," Fern replied bluntly. "I get the feeling he'll hang around for a while, hoping the body will wash up and he'll be there to catch all the excitement."

Regan rolled her eyes. "The only advantage to the news coverage is that the family may hear about her death and come forward. We're trying to help locate them, which is why we wanted to talk to you."

Jack nodded. "I got in touch with Dorie Carpenter this morning. They rented Adele Hopkins the house themselves. Dorie said she tried to get names and numbers for people to contact if there was a problem, but Adele Hopkins never gave her any. Are you aware that the Carpenters met Hopkins right here in your diner? Hopkins overheard them talking and introduced herself."

Fern stared at him. "How did that get by me?" she asked, clearly disappointed in herself.

"I can't imagine," Jack answered teasingly. "This woman was reclusive, but we thought if anyone knew anything about her, it would be you. Dorie said that when they met Mrs. Hopkins here last November, Hopkins said her breakfast had been delicious. We thought she might have come back. She was about sixty. Gray hair. Five foot four. Pug nose."

Fern frowned. "If Hopkins had been here regularly since November, I certainly would have met her and known her name. If she only came in a few times, I could have missed her. I work hard, but I'm not here every minute of every day. I'm not even sure who I'm supposed to be remembering." Fern lowered her voice. "Of course, there are some people you meet once and never forget. This morning a traveling theater group that just arrived in town came in for breakfast. The head of the company is such a pompous phony—and he has the strangest hair! I know I'll never forget him, whether he comes back or not."

"A traveling theater company?" Regan asked. "Where will they perform?"

"Down at The Castle by the Sea. They've got a permit to set up a tent on the lawn from Memorial Day through the end of June. Tomorrow night they're having a cocktail party to introduce themselves and raise money. Mr. Phony Baloney invited me but I'm sure I'll be busy."

The waitress came out with two plates of eggs, toast, and fruit, and placed them in front of Regan and Jack.

"Looks delicious," Regan said.

"Sure does," Jack agreed.

"Don't you know?" Fern asked dramatically. "It's the world premiere of those eggs."

———◆———

"Huh?" Regan asked.

"The theater guy told me that their production would be the *world* premiere of his play. I'm telling you, he really got on my nerves."

20

Devon sat in the cavernous living room of the mansion, guffawing as his actors read aloud the scene from his play that they would perform at the cocktail party. Grandpa arrives at his son and daughter-in-law's new country home to spend the weekend. They are unnerved by his obsession with the gift he brought them—a collection of the sharpest, most expensive brand of kitchen knives, which he'd managed to find on sale. The family had been happy that he recently began taking acting classes. After Grandma died, he'd been spending too much time alone, which worried them. What they didn't expect was that out of the blue he'd begin reciting speeches from his favorite plays, or that he'd grab the biggest knife in his gift set and dangerously wave it around the air for emphasis. His granddaughter is mortified. Her new boyfriend is coming for the weekend. She's convinced that by Sunday night he will have dumped her. Sunday night at the latest.

The scene ended. Devon jumped to his feet and began applauding. "Bravo!" he cried. "Bravo! I couldn't be more proud of you all. My goodness. If you knew all your lines, we could open this show tonight!" he said, with exaggeration.

Five of his actors were smiling. Everyone except Floyd. He didn't look pleased.

Oh no, Devon thought. Here we go and it's only Day One. But he is absolutely marvelous as Grandpa. Putting up with his difficult personality will be worth it in the end. At least I hope. "Floyd," he asked, "do you have any comments about the reading?"

"I need a knife."

"What do you mean?"

Floyd sighed. "I know tomorrow night is just a reading of the scene, and readings don't usually involve props. But it won't work for me unless I'm brandishing a great big knife."

Devon could tell what the other actors were thinking. Everyone was aware of Floyd's volatile reputation. This was just the first story about working with him that they'd relate to their friends in the theater world. "Floyd," Devon said sincerely, "I thought this scene was perfect. I honestly don't think the knife is necessary. When we did the reading in New York—"

"This isn't New York," Floyd interrupted.

"I'm aware of that," Devon said, trying to laugh. "If you are more comfortable using a knife tomorrow night, that's fine. The truck with the props and the scenery won't be here until next week, so I'll go out and buy you a knife that . . ."

"You don't have to do that. There's a big knife at the house where I'm staying. The blade absolutely glistens," he said in a menacing tone. "I'll bring it with me tomorrow night."

"Are you sure, because I can always—"

"I'm always sure," Floyd interrupted.

"Okay then," Devon said. "Let's read the scene one more time . . ."

Floyd shook his head. "You just said it was perfect. We all had a long trip yesterday. I'm tired and so is everyone else. I want to go home and rest."

"You have a point," Devon agreed quickly. "It's probably best to keep the scene fresh. Very well. Floyd, we'll see you back here tomorrow afternoon at 5:30 for the press conference."

Floyd nodded.

"We've gotten a wonderful response from the media on Cape Cod," Devon informed his cast. "After taking questions from the press, the cocktail party will begin at six o'clock, and our reading will be at seven. I just hope this storm has blown away by then! Have a good day, everyone."

The group started to break up.

Floyd walked over to Devon. "I'd like a second copy of the script."

"A second copy?"

"I like to keep one by the bathtub."

"Of course." Devon laughed. "If it falls in, what a mess. A waterlogged script is tough to work with," he chattered.

Floyd just stared at him.

"I have an extra script in the other room," Devon said quickly.

Three minutes later Floyd was back in his car heading home. It was a quick ride. He pulled into the driveway, turned off the car, and hurried up the front steps. He was about to unlock the door when he caught sight of the doorbell. His face lit up. With a big smile on his face, he rang the bell, waited a few minutes, then rang it again. Laughing uncontrollably, he pressed the bell over and over, like an impatient child. I'm enjoying this a lot, he thought. Finally he stopped, put his key in the door, turned the knob, and pushed it open. "Anyone home?" he shouted as he dropped his bag and hurried toward the stairs to the basement.

Adele's heart was beating rapidly. When she heard the doorbell she'd shouted as loud as she could, but when it started ringing incessantly she just knew it was Floyd. He's clinically nuts and gets a thrill out of torturing me.

Floyd came thumping down the steps and flicked on the light. "Miss me?" he asked. "That music is much too loud, don't you think?" He strode across the room to the radio and shut it off. "Much better." He turned and started walking toward her. "You didn't answer my question. Did you miss me?"

"No," Adele spat.

Floyd's eyes widened. "A live wire! I love it." First he untied the ropes around her feet, and then freed her hands. He stood before her, and pointed his finger. "I'm warning you," he said, mimicking the witch from *The Wizard Of Oz,* "Don't try and escape, my little pretty!"

"I wouldn't think of it," Adele answered.

"Good. Now get up."

Her body aching, she struggled to get out of the chair.

"Start up the steps. I'll be right behind you," Floyd instructed.

Adele obeyed, wondering how she was ever going to get away. Grabbing the banister for support, each step she took was an effort.

"Did you know they think you're dead?" he asked from behind her.

"So I heard," she snapped.

"I've always wanted to be at my funeral so I could hear the nice things people say about me," Floyd informed her. "If they have a memorial service for Adele Hopkins, I'll sneak you in."

"Somehow I doubt there will be any service," she answered.

When she reached the top step, she hesitated.

"Go sit on the couch," Floyd demanded.

It's hard to believe that for a brief moment in time, sitting in this room, I dared to believe this guy might be the end to my loneliness. Adele wondered how she could have been so stupid. She sat and noticed that Floyd was fumbling through his bag. "What now?" she asked.

Turning around, he tossed a script in her direction. "You're going to help me learn my lines."

I knew he wanted to torture me, she thought.

21

Regan's best friend, Kit, had been in Boston for two days on a business trip. She was meeting a friend from college for lunch, and planned to drive home to Hartford. I don't relish the trip, she thought, closing her suitcase and rolling it out the door of her hotel room into the lobby. Her cell phone rang. Kit stopped and pulled it out of her purse. "Hey, Meg," she said, recognizing the phone number.

"Kit, I am so sorry. There's a crisis with one of our accounts. I can't leave. Any chance you can stick around this afternoon and we'll meet for an early dinner?"

"Oh Meg, I'd love to see you," Kit answered. "I really would. But right now I'm in the hotel lobby with my suitcase. If it were a nice day I'd walk around and go shopping. But with this rain, I think I'll just get going."

"I'm sorry!" Meg repeated.

"Don't worry about it. We'll get together soon."

Kit hung up her cell phone and shrugged. She'd had nothing but meetings for the last couple of days and it would have been fun to unwind and have a few laughs with a friend. What can you do? she thought as she proceeded to the valet and handed him the ticket for her car.

"It'll be right out," he said.

Twenty minutes later an attendant pulled the car around. I guess that's what he means by "right out," Kit thought as her bag was loaded into the trunk. The attendant then opened her door. She handed him a tip as she was getting in the car.

"Thank you. Please visit us again soon," he mumbled.

Kit put on her seat belt and adjusted the rearview mirror. As she started to pull out of the driveway, she felt a case of the blahs. She was single and had no big plans for the weekend. Regan is so lucky she met Jack, Kit thought as she pulled into traffic. My father would do anything to help me meet a guy, except get kidnapped. Regan's father, Luke, had had no choice. He'd been kidnapped in New York City, and Jack Reilly, head of the NYPD Major Case Squad, had been called in. He was so perfect, he even had the same last name as Regan. On top of that, he helped save Luke's life. Kit braked as she approached a red light.

A moment later the light turned green. She pressed on the gas just as a man ran from the sidewalk in front of her car. "You idiot!" Kit screamed, slamming on the brakes, barely missing him. He kept running and made it to the other side of the street. Her heart beating wildly, Kit pressed on the gas again. That's definitely not road rage, she told herself. What a day this has been. I'd love to talk to Regan right now, but I'm not going to call.

Regan was away with Jack this weekend celebrating their first anniversary. She was sure they'd be relishing their quiet time alone and she didn't want to disturb them. Their lives were hectic and they'd been looking forward to a weekend free of obligations. Not that Regan would feel like it was an obligation to talk to me, Kit thought. They were best friends and Kit was sure they'd remain that way for life.

As Kit drove along, she felt increasingly down in the dumps. Just the sound of Regan's voice cheers me up, she thought. But I can't call. It's her anniversary weekend.

Two miles later, Kit changed her mind. I'll call and if she answers the phone, I'll make it quick. I'll wish them a happy anniversary, even though it's not until Sunday.

Kit's cell phone was connected to the Bluetooth in her car. She leaned over, pressed a button, then pressed Regan's name when it came up on the screen. As the connection was made, Kit put her hand back on the steering wheel.

After two rings, Regan picked up. "Hi, Kit!"

"Regan, hi."

"What's the matter?"

"Nothing!" Kit insisted. "I'm fine. I just wanted to say a quick hello. I'm heading home from my business trip to Boston."

"How was it?"

"A little stressful. But it's over. Listen, how is it down there? The rain isn't coming through the roof or anything like that, I hope."

"No, the roof's not leaking," Regan laughed, "but—"

"Listen, Regan, I don't want to hold you," Kit interrupted. "I just thought I'd say hi, so have a good time . . ."

"Kit!" Regan said. "Why are you hanging up? You didn't let me finish my answer."

"Sorry."

"Do you have a couple minutes?"

"I just got in the car. I've got plenty of time."

Quickly Regan explained their day.

"Are you kidding?" Kit asked. "And those ladies and the caretaker are staying at the house with you tonight? I can't believe it. I pictured you two having a romantic weekend."

"That was the plan. What are you doing this weekend?"

"Nothing really," Kit answered. "I'll go to the gym . . ."

"You're just leaving Boston now?"

"Yes."

"Drive to the Cape."

"What?"

"Come down for the night. Although you might not ever speak to me again. As a matter of fact, I'm sure you'll never speak to me again. This will be the end of our friendship, but come on down anyway. We're having a potluck dinner."

Kit laughed. Regan knows me so well, she thought, as her eyes grew misty. "Are you sure?"

"Yes! Maybe you can help us figure out who Adele Hopkins is and where she came from."

"I'm sure I'll crack the case wide open," Kit answered. "What's your address down there? I'll plug it into my GPS."

"Pond Road in Chatwich. We're the next-to-the-last house on the left. If we're not there for some reason, but our visitors are, good luck."

"Thanks, Regan. I'll just stay one night. When I was your maid of honor last year, I never thought I'd be with you and Jack on your first-anniversary weekend getaway."

"The more the merrier. If you see someone along the way who you'd like to invite, by all means feel free."

"Goodbye, Regan!" Kit said.

"Goodbye!"

Kit pressed the disconnect button. I know I'll never find another friend like her, she thought, her spirits lifted. It doesn't sound like Adele Hopkins had any friends at all. The poor woman.

22

Nora Regan Reilly spent the morning working on her next book. At lunchtime she brought a sandwich to her desk, printed the pages she had just written, and as she ate, read them over. Pen in hand, she scribbled minor changes. She had already made most of her major revisions on the computer. One of her friends who owned a bookstore remarked that computers were great, but writers who use them no longer had true first drafts of their manuscripts. Thanks to the delete button, the original versions of their work never see the light of day. Nora had joked that that was probably the way most writers wanted it.

After making her corrections, Nora went back downstairs and turned on the kettle. Waiting for the water to boil, she peered out the kitchen window. The rain was still coming down in sheets.

What a day, she thought, then smiled. I wonder if the wedding cake has been delivered yet. Last year she had wrapped that top layer so carefully before storing it in the freezer, following instructions she'd found on the internet, which required plastic bags, plastic wrap, a vacuum bag, a box, and more plastic. Yet nearly every reader's comment she'd read on those wedding cake websites said that no matter what they'd done, their anniversary cake tasted lousy. One woman wrote that she and her husband took a taste and threw the rest away. As long as Regan and Jack take one bite of the cake this Sunday, I'll be happy, Nora decided as the kettle started to shriek. She was dying to find out if all that plastic had been worth it.

Just last year at this time, Nora thought again, as she prepared her tea. Just last year. I can picture everything. She sighed. A couple of minutes later she found herself sitting in the den, watching the video of Regan's wedding day.

Nora smiled at the scenes of Regan getting ready with the bridesmaids, Regan getting out of the limo at the church, the bridesmaids coming down the aisle. Then the music stopped and all was quiet. When Regan and Luke came from the side of the vestibule and stepped into view at the back of the church, Nora reached for her hankie and dabbed her eyes. The congregation rose. The Trumpet Voluntary in D filled the air, and the two people she loved most in this world started up the aisle. By the time they were halfway to the altar, Nora's eyes had welled with tears. But it was the sight of a beaming Jack, reaching out his hand for Regan, that sent the tears spilling down her cheeks. "Thank God!" she cried, shaking her head, and wiping her eyes. "Thank you God," she whispered.

"Having fun?"

Nora jumped.

Luke was standing in the doorway, smiling from ear to ear. "I wish Regan could see this. And I don't mean the video."

"Luke!" Nora protested. Flustered, she dabbed her eyes again and tried to laugh. "It's very emotional. I hadn't watched the video in so long."

"It sounds like you never thought Regan would get married."

"No—" Nora waved her hand. "You know I don't mean that. I never thought that she'd find someone as wonderful as Jack."

"Oh I see."

"It's true!"

"She has me to thank."

"She knows, Luke, she knows!" Nora said, trying to regain her composure. "As long as you're here, why don't you sit down and watch with me for a few minutes?"

"I'm hungry. I thought I'd stop home for lunch."

"Five minutes, I promise. Then I'll make you a sandwich."

The phone rang.

"Saved by the bell!" Luke said happily as Nora reached for the phone.

"Hello."

"Hi, Nora, this is Eileen Reilly."

"Hello, Eileen, how have you been?"

"Pretty good. And you?"

"Fine," Nora answered. By now Luke had escaped to the kitchen and was making a sandwich.

"With Regan and Jack's anniversary upon us, I've been thinking that we don't see you enough. When the kids get back, why don't the six of us make a date to have dinner in the city? We can toast them together."

"That's a marvelous idea," Nora answered. "We'd love that. I'm sure Regan and Jack are having a wonderful anniversary weekend at your place on the Cape."

"Oh," Eileen said. "I guess you haven't spoken to Regan."

"No I haven't," Nora answered quickly. "I didn't think I'd hear from her this weekend."

"Well, the only reason Jack called me . . ." Eileen began.

Nora listened as Eileen filled her in on what had happened to her neighbor's tenant.

"... So I told Jack we had a key to the Carpenters' house they could use. Dorie and I keep a copy of each other's keys in case of emergencies."

"What did they find?" Nora asked.

"I don't know."

Nora was stunned. "You don't?"

"Jack hasn't called back yet. I'm sure he will later. I didn't want to bother him in case they're still working with the police."

If Regan and Jack were staying at my house and something like this happened, Nora thought, I wouldn't be able to help myself from calling every five minutes, police or no police. "Well, Eileen, this is quite a shock. It's such a terrible shame about that woman."

"It certainly is. And our caretaker is just the sweetest kid. I feel so sorry for him. He's devastated."

Nora remembered a literature class she'd taken in college. The professor said that some of the saddest feelings people experience are when they think about "what might have been."

"It's understandable he's so upset," Nora agreed. "I'll call Regan later this afternoon and check in."

"Let's talk again next week and set up that dinner date."

Nora hung up and carried the phone into the kitchen.

"What happened?" Luke asked. "Are you okay, honey?"

"Wait till you hear this," she said, recounting to Luke what Eileen had told her, then she hurriedly dialed Regan's cell number. "I can't believe that woman was swept out to sea. It's so sad. I know you said not to call Regan, but this is different. I just want to know what's going on . . ."

Luke nodded. Swept out to sea, he thought. Being a funeral director, he knew how painful it was for families when there'd be no grave site to visit, nor ashes to hold dear.

23

———◆———

Reed jumped up from the couch when Olivia came breezing into the apartment. "My morning was fine," he answered quickly. "I've been preparing for my meeting this afternoon."

Olivia came over, put her arms around his neck, and kissed him. "We closed the office early. After you get back, we have the whole weekend together. Finally! I can't stand all these business trips!"

Olivia was new to Boston when she met Reed. The start-up technology company she worked for was opening offices all around the world, which meant that her job involved constant travel. Boston was the latest city her company had targeted. Olivia's boss promised if she relocated to Boston she wouldn't have to go on the road as much, which greatly relieved her. She moved into a club downtown, intending to look for an apartment, but never had time. The traveling was less, but still a burden. Then she met Reed. They fell in love so fast. He convinced her to move in with him.

Reed was trying to focus. He was still reeling from what Ellen had written about him. "We'll have a wonderful weekend," he agreed.

"Sit, sit," Olivia told him. "I don't want to interrupt your work. How about if I fix us lunch?"

"I'd love that," he lied. His guts were churning. I'm going to lose her, he thought, as she hurried away, humming a tune as she hung up her coat. I can't let that happen. He ran his hand through his hair and felt himself sweating.

Shouldn't Ellen be happy with all her success? Can't she just leave me alone? Is she going to keep this up forever?

He was afraid she was. Like a dog with a bone, Ellen was never going to let go.

Reed could barely eat, which Olivia noticed.

"Can I fix you something else?" she asked. "This quiche was—"

"No," he said quickly, then smiled. "I'm so preoccupied by this meeting."

"We'll have a nice dinner," Olivia said, clearing the plates. "I'll leave you in peace and go downstairs to the gym. I'm so glad I don't have to go out in the rain!"

Reed went back to his computer. Olivia straightened up the kitchen, then went into the bedroom. It was comforting to have her around. Ten minutes later she sailed past him in her workout clothes. "See you later, darling." She disappeared out the door, a trace of her perfume lingering in the air.

Reed didn't move a muscle. The apartment felt so empty without her. He'd lied to Olivia about the meeting. There was no meeting. He wanted her to think that at least something was happening in his career.

He spent twenty minutes surfing the web before Olivia burst through the door. Quickly he looked up.

"Reed, my mother just called my cell phone!" she said excitedly. "Daddy isn't feeling well again. My mother's afraid he might have another heart attack. They're on their way to the hospital."

Reed jumped up and hurried toward her. "What can I do?"

She looked up at him. It broke his heart to see how sad her eyes were. She'd obviously been crying. "I'm afraid I'm going to have to fly home," she said, her voice cracking. "I'm sorry about our weekend."

"Don't be silly," Reed said. "Let me go with you."

Olivia shook her head. "No, that's not going to work. My mother is so private and formal and old-world. I think it would be better if I went alone. This isn't the time for you to meet my parents."

Reed hugged her. "I'm sorry that hasn't happened yet. At Christmas I had to go visit my mother . . ."

"Oh, I know," Olivia said. "And we had those plans to go away for New Year's, so there wasn't time to visit each other's families. The time has gone so fast!" She started crying. "I'm so worried about my father."

"Let me come with you," Reed suggested. "I'll fly with you to Atlanta, then fly back. You shouldn't be alone."

"No," Olivia insisted. "You have that meeting this afternoon. I'll call the airlines and book a flight. I hope that there aren't too many delays with all this rain."

"At least let me drive you to the airport."

"No. I want to leave as soon as possible. Concentrate on your presentation. You've had enough disappointments lately . . ."

All thanks to Ellen, he thought angrily.

"We'll have reason to celebrate if you get this project off the ground," she said, daintily wiping her eyes.

Reed stared at her. She was so beautiful and at this moment looked so vulnerable. He cupped her face in his hands. "You are in my life. Believe me, Livvy, I need no other reason to celebrate."

She nodded. "Me too. I'd better pack." She hurried past him into the bedroom.

Standing in the living room, Reed shook his head. He felt helpless. He hated seeing Olivia so upset. We belong together. I should have proposed already but didn't want to seem too anxious. I will when she comes back. She loves me and has stood by my side when other women would have walked away. And now, with her father sick, how much more can she take? If she hears about what Ellen wrote today . . .

Reed's jaw tightened. If she does, she does. But there's one thing I'm going to make certain, he thought darkly. There will be nothing for her to hear about again.

24

Regan was finishing up the conversation with her mother as she and Jack got in the car outside Fern's. Or at least she thought she was. "I promise . . . Yes, the neighbors are on their way down from Boston . . . It is remarkable that they knew nothing about a woman they rented their house to . . . Jack will have his office trace the license plate once we get in the garage . . . I promise I'll let you know . . ."

By the time she hung up, they were halfway back to the Reilly home. "I get the feeling my mother is in shock that you haven't called your mother back."

"I don't have anything to tell her."

"That has nothing to do with it."

Jack smiled. "I, for one, can't believe Fern didn't know this woman. Hopkins must have placed herself in solitary confinement."

"Avoiding Ginny and Fran I can understand," Regan said. "Not Fern's diner. If those two find out they were living alone on a block with someone who might have been hiding out from the bad guys, they won't be pleased. I can just hear them now."

"They're right, though," Jack said. "For all we know Hopkins could have been dealing drugs."

"I doubt it," Regan said. "Not with all those apology cards on the table."

A few minutes later they were passing Ginny and Fran's home. The front window was still covered with plastic. "I'm surprised they're not back yet." Jack commented.

"Uh-oh," Regan said. "Look what's ahead." A news van was parked in front of the Carpenters' house. "That reporter Fern was talking about must still be here."

"Let's get into the house as fast as we can," Jack said. "It would help if they ever paved the end of this road," he added, slowing down to avoid the holes and bumps his parents had been complaining about for years.

By the time he turned into their driveway, the reporter and his cameraman had hightailed it to their property. He and Regan both got out of the car, only to have a microphone stuck in their faces as they hurried up the walk.

"Sir, do you live here?" the reporter asked, moving quickly beside them.

"It's my parents' home," Jack answered, Regan's hand in his as they continued toward the house.

"I understand it was your family's caretaker who found Adele Hopkins on the beach and left her there. Can I get your comments on what a terrible mistake that was?"

You just lost him, pal, Regan thought as Jack's face tightened.

"The whole situation is a tragedy," Jack replied, his tone curt. "If you don't mind." Key in hand, he unlocked the door, pushed it open, and followed Regan inside.

The reporter continued shouting questions after they closed the door. "Do you think Hopkins was still alive? Did you know her? . . ."

"Ohhhh," Jack grunted as he and Regan headed toward the

kitchen. "There are a lot of good reporters on the Cape. I don't know where this one came from."

"I just hope he's gone by the time Skip gets back," Regan said, then frowned. "How long can it take to buy a piece of wood?"

25

Devon stood at the kitchen door waving goodbye and watching as Floyd raced to his car and tore down the driveway. If only a good long soak in a tub would calm you down, Devon thought frantically, I'd draw your bath myself.

Devon finally closed the door, his mind reeling. When he turned around, the rest of his cast were standing together at the other end of the huge kitchen, their faces solemn. Oh no, Devon thought. It's going to be a long, hot summer.

Hadley Wilder, the actor playing the father, took a step forward. "Devon, we need to speak to you."

Devon opened his mouth but before he could get a word out, Annie, the sweet little actress playing the ingenue, tore into him. "How can you possibly expect me to sit next to Floyd during the reading tomorrow night if he has a big knife whose 'blade glistens' in his hand? It's much too dangerous!" she cried.

Brandon, who played Annie's boyfriend in the play, patted her back. "It's okay, Annie," he said comfortingly. "We won't let that happen."

The first cast romance ignites before my eyes, Devon thought. With such a small group, it will probably be the only one. I hope. Several years ago, in one of Devon's off-off-

Broadway productions in New York, the two leading actors fell in and out of love during the run of the show. It was bad enough they had to see each other at the theater, but at least everyone went home at night. If the show had been on the road, it would have been a nightmare. These two better continue to get along, he thought. "Believe me . . ." Devon began.

Apparently Annie had more to say. "It's not as if I don't fully appreciate the opportunity to be in this play and to act with the legendary Floyd Wellington. I know I will learn so much from him. He never plays it safe onstage, which is admirable. As an actress, I know I have to take more risks." She paused. "But he's a little crazy! I will not risk life and limb, even for the chance to work with him!"

What about the chance to work with me? Devon wondered, his feelings hurt.

"No, Annie," Brandon was saying, "You are so beautiful and . . ."

At least the initial audiences won't have a hard time believing these two are infatuated with one another, Devon thought. He opened his mouth to speak, but it was too late. Hadley had the floor again.

"Devon, it's essential that you find a fake knife for tomorrow's performance. I've been in dozens and dozens of shows over the years, and there has *never* been a real gun, or a real knife, or a real sword onstage!" he said forcefully. "I understand you want to indulge Floyd, and the prop truck isn't here yet, but you've got to find a solution."

Now it was Martha's turn. "Last month at a theater in Europe where a friend of mine was working an actor picked up a knife during a scene, expecting it to be a fake, of course, and stuck it in his mouth. It was a real knife. Someone had switched the prop knife!"

Chuck, the actor who played Martha and Hadley's son, blinked. "Is the actor okay?"

"Yes. A few stitches closed the wound in his cheek and he was back onstage the next night."

Chuck pumped his fist. "That's what I'd do!" he boasted, then asked eagerly, "Did they find out who made the switch?"

"Last I heard they were taking DNA samples of the cast and crew."

"If you please," Devon said quickly. "I understand your concerns, believe me. I feel the same way."

"Then why didn't you tell him he couldn't bring a real knife?" Annie asked, Brandon's hand now on her shoulder.

Someday you might understand, Devon thought. If you ever have investors breathing down your neck and your whole world is at stake. "As you can see, he just left," Devon began, pointing at the door. "What I plan to do now is call and find out if I can get the prop knives sent to us overnight. That would be the best-case scenario. Floyd has seen those knives and approved of them. But even if I know they're on their way, I still won't sleep tonight unless I have a backup. I will contact the other theaters on the Cape and see if any one of them has a suitable knife in their prop room. If not, I will find a store somewhere on the Cape or in Boston . . ." Devon sighed. A second later he straightened up and squared his shoulders. "I would never ever have allowed him to use a knife that could possibly endanger any one of you!"

For a moment, the actors seemed to be placated. But it was a brief moment.

"What if the knives he'll use in the show don't arrive and Floyd refuses any other knife you find?" Chuck blurted. "Then what?"

"Then I will fire him!" Devon barked.

The room was silent. "I will fire him," Devon repeated, not quite believing that he had uttered those words. "But it won't come to that. No matter how unusual the experience might be to work with Floyd, he is still a consummate professional. He has always been committed one hundred percent to any role he plays, so much so that he's been known to live the role offstage."

Annie rolled her eyes. "I'm glad he's not staying here with us," she said with a laugh.

A few of the actors chuckled.

"My good friends," Devon said with a relieved smile on his face, raising his arms. "This is life in the theater! Unpredictable, crazy, but in the end, thrilling! We may encounter problems along the way, but we're going to put on a great show! Now go relax, rest, call your loved ones, whatever floats your boat."

"Are we going out to dinner?" Brandon asked. "You said you'd made a reservation . . ."

The last thing on my mind right now is food, Devon thought. "Yes, I have," he answered, "at a marvelous Italian restaurant. Let's all meet back here at seven thirty. We'll have a wonderful meal, we'll laugh, we'll enjoy, and I promise you, I will have in my possession a faux knife that even Floyd Wellington will think is real!"

It took a few minutes, but the actors dispersed. Devon went into the room off the kitchen he was using as an office, and sank into the chair at his desk. That convinced *me*, he thought. I knew I shouldn't let Floyd brandish a knife, especially in front of the press, who would be sitting a few feet away from the actors. Staging the reading was risky enough. Devon had wanted people to get a taste of the very beginning of the rehearsal process. Hopefully it would hook them, they'd feel connected to the production, and they'd come back with all their friends to see the fully produced show when it opened. But what if they didn't like the play in the first place? They'd never come back and word would spread that the show wasn't worth the price of admission. I have all that to worry about and now I have to spend my precious time worrying about finding a fake knife that is suitable for Floyd?

Devon reached for the phone. I'm going to make this work, he told himself with determination. I have to. If Floyd insists on using his own knife, I'll play Grandpa myself.

Even though I'm much too youthful.

26

To be or not to be!" Floyd thundered, waving a large kitchen knife around the air. "That is the question." He paused and stomped his foot. "Line please."

Adele didn't need to look at the script. "Whether 'tis nobler—"

"I got it," Floyd said impatiently. He took a moment, then continued. "Whether 'tis nobler in the mind to suffer the slings and arrows of outrageous fortune, or take arms against opposing trouble. . . ."

"Mom, Grandpa is freaking me out," Adele read. "Make him stop."

Floyd shook his head. "Adele!" he shouted. "Would you mind reading those lines with a little more passion? How can I really learn my part if you give me nothing to work with? *Nothing!*" He charged toward her.

Adele swallowed. He was two feet away, his face enraged. "I'll try harder," she promised. "I've never acted before."

"And you never will!" he screamed.

I hope he means because I'll never be hired, Adele thought. He hadn't tied her up, but she didn't dare try to escape. "If you don't mind," she said to him, "I feel a little weak. Could I have a cup of tea? I never did get to finish the cup you made me this morning. I'd also like to use the ladies' room."

"Oh, fine," he said with disgust. "You have no commitment to your craft."

"What craft? You just said I'll never act."

"Any craft! Whatever field, whatever endeavor in life, nothing happens until one commits!"

Commit, Adele thought. I'd like to commit you to an institution for the criminally insane.

"Did you ever have a job?" Floyd demanded.

"Yes I did."

"Did you commit yourself to your work?"

"Yes," Adele answered. "I put my heart and soul into my work every single day."

"Good! Good! Then you enjoyed it! It made you happy!"

More than you will ever know, Adele thought. I was such a fool. "Can I please—"

"Yes, yes. Go ahead. The topic obviously bores you."

"No it doesn't," Adele protested as she slowly got up from the couch. It just makes me incredibly sad, she thought.

"Ten-minute break," Floyd announced. "But first, tell me. What do you think of the play?"

"It's funny," Adele answered, then began to walk slowly across the room. Her whole body ached. Floyd was right behind her.

"Funny? Of course it's funny!" he fumed. "Do you think I'd accept a part in a play that's considered a comedy if it weren't funny?"

"No. I know you're much too smart to do something like that," Adele answered.

"The director annoys me, but I guess I'll have to put up with him."

She'd reached the bathroom door. "May I go inside, please?"

"Yes. I'll wait right here," he announced, pointing at the floor with the knife. "Don't try anything stupid."

27

After speaking to Jack, Dorie Carpenter called her husband on his cell phone and left a message. "Dan, when you finish your workout, please come home right away. Don't worry. Love you, 'bye."

Then she had run into the bedroom and packed a bag for the two of them. She turned on the TV and was horrified that the story of Adele Hopkins's death had already hit the wires. At least they don't know how idiotic her landlords are, Dorie thought. Not yet, anyway. Though it was obvious the press was looking for more details. She quickly called Jack again and asked if it was possible to avoid telling people they knew nothing about Adele Hopkins.

A mile away, Dan was leaving the gym, a smile on his face. He'd exercised hard, relaxed in the steam room, and enjoyed a nice hot shower. His endorphins were flowing and all felt right with the world. The pouring rain didn't bother him in the least.

As he was leaving work yesterday, Dan had waved good night to his boss, who replied by asking him to come in and sit down. His heart in his mouth, Dan took a seat at the foot of his boss's massive antique desk.

"Dan, I just want to say how proud of you I am," Mickey

McPhee III began. "You work hard, but even more important, you have good judgment. That's what I like about you. In a crisis, I know that I can count on you to do the right thing. I know that you will always make our company proud. I know that you will never do anything that would reflect poorly on McPhee and You, the advertising agency my grandfather started eighty-two years ago tomorrow." He lifted his arm and pointed backward with his thumb to the portrait above his desk of a smiling, muttonchopped, Mickey McPhee the First.

Dan had nodded and murmured his thanks. The reputation of McPhee and You was a touchy subject. One of their award-winning copywriters had been caught stealing from the collection basket at his church. The local papers had gotten hold of the story and run with it, gleefully citing ads the dishonest employee had created that stressed trust in a product. "Your grandfather was a brilliant man," Dan said reverently.

"They don't make them like Grandpa anymore," Mickey said sadly. "That's why we will always honor him on April seventh. I know there's been a lot of pressure around here lately. My wife thinks we should all come to the office tomorrow and get things done, but I told her no—April seventh will always be a day to honor Mickey McPhee." He clapped his hands once, then stood. "Enjoy your day off, say a prayer for Grandpa, and come back to work Monday raring to go. I hope to have the signed contract back from the folks over at Sinclair's by then."

"I am very excited about that project," Dan had said eagerly, always anxious to please. Sinclair's was a department store in Boston that wanted to liven up its image. "See you Monday."

He'd hurried home to tell Dorie about his chat with the boss.

Dan smiled at the memory as he got in his car and reached for a Bruce Springsteen CD. As he backed out of his parking space, "Born to Run" started to blare from the speakers. In the three minutes it took him to drive home, Dan sang at the top of his lungs. Anyone who knew him would have been shocked at the sight of the quiet, slightly nervous Dan letting it rip. When he pulled into the driveway, he stayed in the car, continuing to sing and gesture until he and Bruce wrapped things up, Dan pounding the steering wheel with a fierce passion as the song ended.

Getting out of his car, he had no idea his bubble was about to burst. He opened his umbrella, hurried up the walk, and went in the front door of his house. He hadn't even put the umbrella in its stand when Dorie came running down the stairs.

"Don't take off your coat!" she cried. "What were you doing in the driveway? Didn't you get my message?"

"Huh?" Dan asked, his boyish face confused. He ran his hand through his wavy reddish brown hair. "I was just . . ."

"Never mind. We have to get down to the Cape."

"The Cape?" His eyebrows were now almost vertical.

"Yes, the Cape. I'm afraid I have bad news. I'll tell you in the car. I packed a bag for us so we can leave right away."

"No, Dorie. Tell me now."

"Jack Reilly called. He and Regan and are down there for the weekend. Adele Hopkins was swept out to sea.

Dan's eyes widened and his stomach dropped. "What happened?"

"I'll explain to you in the car," she repeated. "We have to get down there. Jack and Regan are going to help us try and figure out where Adele came from and who to contact."

Swallowing hard, Dan said, "Surely there is something in the house that will identify her, right?" he asked hopefully.

"Jack and Regan have already been in the house with the police. Mrs. Hopkins must have had her wallet with her. We have to get down there and unlock the garage so Jack can trace her license plate."

"Dorie!" Dan cried. "How could we have been so stupid? If my boss ever found out that we rented our house to a complete stranger and didn't ask for references . . ."

"It was twenty-five thousand dollars cash, honey," Dorie reminded him. She picked up a bag by the umbrella stand. "Let's go."

"I just hope Mickey McPhee III never hears about this," Dan lamented.

"It's been on the news."

"What?!"

"They're just reporting that she drowned and the neighbors don't know anything about her. They don't know yet that we don't either. That's why we have to hurry. If the Reillys find out who Hopkins was, the media will never have to know that we were so naïve that we never checked her references."

"We lacked judgment!" Dan cried as they hurried out the door and down the walk. "That's what McPhee counts on me for."

"I know. You just told me yesterday! Get in the other side," Dorie ordered. "I'll drive."

As they pulled out of the driveway, Dan was shaking his head. "I knew it was a mistake. I just knew it."

"Dan, the poor woman is dead! Think about that for a minute."

"I feel terrible for her. But what if it turns out she had a crazy past and we put our neighbors in danger? How is that going to look?"

They rode down to the Cape in silence.

28

Adele eyed her wet clothes that were thrown over the side of the bathtub. To think that the only reason I set foot outside the house this morning was to pick up my computer at the repair shop, she mused. My laptop was finally ready and I was anxious to get it back. So anxious that I leave the house in the middle of a raging storm, impulsively decide to check my boat, and the next thing I know I'm being held captive by a lunatic. Those jerks who spread viruses on the internet should know the trouble they cause.

Adele tiptoed across the bathroom to the tub. If by any chance her cell phone still worked she'd try sending a text message to 911. All in caps. With lots of exclamation points so they'd know she meant business. She had no idea if 911 accepted text messages but she'd give it her best shot. Slowly she unzipped the right front pocket of her jacket and slid her hand inside. A chill ran through her body. Her cell phone, keys, and small wallet were gone. She pulled out a jagged piece of paper and stared in horror at the wild scrawling. OH ADELE. YOU'RE SUCH A SILLY WOMAN!

Floyd pounded on the door. "Your zipper is very noisy. I've

never been so insulted in my entire life," he yelled, then started to laugh. "You think I'd be stupid enough to let you in there alone if your cell phone were still in your jacket pocket! I've got news, my dear. That phone is at the bottom of Cape Cod Bay." He paused. "Where everyone thinks you are."

29

House Junction was crowded with shoppers. In the lumber aisle, Skip had to wait twenty minutes to get help from a salesman. He ordered the proper size plywood—which would be wrapped in plastic and available for pickup at the back door of the store—and set out to find the other items he needed. Ginny and Fran followed him through the aisles as he threw assorted odds and ends into a basket. Finally they got in a long line for the register. When it was their turn to pay, the store's computers went down.

The sound of customers' grumblings and complaints filled the air.

"This place should be called Madhouse Junction," Ginny observed.

Fran nodded. "I'm exhausted."

Skip just stared off into space.

Moments later, the sound of someone tapping a microphone came over the loudspeaker and a man's voice boomed through the store. "Ladies and gentlemen, we appreciate your patience. Our computer system is down but hopefully not for long. This has happened in the past . . ."

The cashier at their register looked at Ginny and rolled her eyes. "In the past?" she whispered. "Try yesterday."

"How long before?" Ginny began.

"Good news, folks! The computers are up and running!" the announcer blurted excitedly, as though he were calling a horse race. "Have a good day everyone and please come back and visit us again. Make House Junction your . . ." The microphone started screeching and whining, then was clicked off.

"Give it a rest," the cashier muttered as she began to scan the items in Skip's basket.

Forty-five minutes later the threesome was bouncing down Pond Road, the large piece of wood jigging around the back of the truck. They could see a news van parked in front of the Carpenters' house.

"Oh no," Skip muttered as he turned into Fran and Ginny's driveway.

"Don't worry, Skip," Fran said. "We won't let anyone bother you."

"I'd go home right now if I hadn't promised to board up your window. I'm not going to back out of that. But as soon as I finish, I'd better get out of here." He opened his door.

"Skip, no!" Ginny protested as they got out of the car.

In the distance they could see a reporter and cameraman running toward them.

"Let's get inside," Fran ordered, her keys in hand.

Quickly they ran up the steps, into the house, and shut the door just as the Carpenters' old convertible rode past their property. Ginny peeked through the plastic covering the broken front window. The reporter had reversed his course, and was now chasing the Carpenters' car back down the block. "Skip, look. The coast is clear!"

"Maybe for now," he said as he started back outside. "But it won't be for long."

30

Ellen was trying to be patient, but the customers she was helping had been in the store for what seemed like forever. The mother and daughter had stopped in and decided that pillows would make great gifts for the daughter's eight bridesmaids. It soon became clear that the twentysomething bride-to-be was the type who would obsess over every last detail of her big day until it happened. Then she'd obsess over everything that went wrong.

The wedding wasn't until August but she wanted to get the pillows ordered. "I'd like something about friendship written on the pillows," she said. "But I have a different kind of relationship with each of my bridesmaids. Nancy I've known since kindergarten, Carin I met when we were Brownies together, Lindsey I met at work a few years ago and we really hit it off. I want every pillow to be very special. I'm afraid I don't know what to do."

Ellen nodded. "You really don't have to decide today. I've got an idea. If you don't know each bridesmaid's favorite color, why not find out what it is? It might be nice to order the pillows in your friends' favorite colors. Then look for quotes about friendship and see what you'd like to use. You can let us know.

The wedding is four months away," she said with a big smile. "There's plenty of time."

The girl looked at Ellen with a perplexed expression. "I know all their favorite colors. How could you be friends with someone and not know their favorite color?"

Ellen shrugged and pretended to laugh. "Beats me."

"My problem," the girl continued, "is that one of my friends has two favorite colors and another has three." She shook her head as if she had the weight of the world on her Burberry-covered shoulders. "I need to get this done today."

Forty-five agonizing minutes later the order was complete. The bride crossed off the last name on her list. "You say they'll be ready in two weeks?"

"Yes," Ellen answered, as she watched the bride unzip her soft leather briefcase and pull out a Preparing for Your Wedding book. It looked to Ellen like a battle plan. The bride pursed her lips, turned to the page for April 21, made a notation, then sighed. "There's so much to get done. It's all so stressful. I want everything to be perfect."

"Don't worry, dear," her mother said soothingly. "Everything will be perfect."

When they left the store, Ellen ran to the back room, where Pippy was at the computer. "Uggh," she cried. "I just decided that if I ever get married, I'm going to elope. Definitely elope." She laughed and poured herself a cup of coffee. When she turned around, Pippy was frowning. "What's the matter, Pippy?"

"Read this e-mail," Pippy said, handing her a sheet of paper. "I've been dying for you to get finished out there."

Ellen's eyes darted back and forth as she read the angry words from the person who had been coached by a woman named Adele Hopkins. "This Adele Hopkins would be a hundred and ten years old?"

Pippy nodded. "I feel terrible. I wrote the lady back and apologized, but she says she'll never read another e-mail from us."

"Don't feel bad, Pippy. This woman is no angel. She did say she wanted to break her rowing coach's nose. That's not very nice."

"I know, but still."

The rain was beating down on the roof. "I can't believe Mrs. Hopkins is dead," Ellen said softly.

"Me neither."

"I would love to find out who sent back that slashed pillow."

"Whoever it was must have been really mad at Mrs. Hopkins."

Ellen shivered. "It's creepy to think that someone is enraged enough to take a knife and start slashing a gift, and then go to all the trouble to send it back!"

"It is creepy," Pippy agreed. "You know, Ellen, I don't want to tell you what to do, but maybe you should be careful about what you say online"—she paused—"especially about your ex-boss. I can't help it, I worry."

"You're right," Ellen said, taking a sip of her coffee. "I was surprised when someone asked about him today during the web chat. You'll have to admit, I haven't talked about him lately. From now on I'll avoid any mention of him, I promise. Time to move on."

"Good."

"Reed's a chicken," Ellen said. "He'll never do anything. You don't have to worry."

"I told you I can't help it." Pippy made a face. "What do you want to do tonight?"

"I'm kind of tired," Ellen said. "With all this rain, I would just like to go home and relax. Did you want to go out?"

"No. The only thing I was thinking about was going to get a manicure at the mall. We have that event tomorrow night."

"The Traveling Thespians," Ellen said dramatically. "The things we do to drum up business."

"I bet we'll have fun," Pippy said. "It'll be a chance to meet people. We've been working so hard for six months now and have hardly gone out. After the cocktail party we should treat ourselves to a really nice dinner somewhere."

"I'm just kidding," Ellen said. "I am looking forward to the evening. Another thing I forgot to tell you. I spoke to my grandmother last night and told her we're going to the cocktail party. She asked who was in the cast. I didn't remember and got out the invitation. We're both so excited that I'm going to see Floyd Wellington again."

"Who is Floyd Wellington?"

"He's a famous theater actor. When I was a little girl and visited my grandmother in New York, she'd always take me to Broadway shows. I got old Floyd's autograph outside the stage door after we saw him in a play. He was so charming. I was probably nine years old."

"It sounds like you have a crush on him," Pippy teased.

Ellen waved her hand. "No. He's in his sixties now. I just remember his taking a minute to talk to me when he signed my playbill. Then he shook my hand. I was a little kid and he made me feel like he really cared about me." She laughed. "If I get the chance to talk to him tomorrow night, I'll have to tell him that story."

"You'll get the chance," Pippy said. "I bet he asks you out on a date."

"No way!" Ellen said as she went out to the showroom to greet their latest customers.

31

This is insane," Dan croaked as he and Dorie drove past the Reillys' house and turned left into a little section of land in front of the house that they'd paved over for extra parking space. "That reporter is chasing us like we just escaped from prison. I don't want to be on camera! What's with him?"

"He smells a story," Dorie replied as she quickly turned off the car. "Let's make a run for it. If we get caught I'll say something fast."

The walkway to the house was right outside the passenger door. The minute Dan's feet hit the ground he took off like a shot. Dorie wasn't so lucky. She had to go around the back of the car, where she came face to face with the wild-eyed newsman.

"Are you Mrs. Carpenter?" he asked, sticking the microphone in her face.

"Yes," Dorie answered. "If you don't mind I'm getting soaked." She turned and started hurrying up the path to the house.

"What can you tell us about Adele Hopkins?" the reporter asked as once again he and his cameraman struggled to keep up with a reluctant interviewee. "She's such a tragic figure. All those apology cards. They're probably still inside. Do you think I could have one?"

"No, you may not!" Dorie exploded. "It's appalling that you would even ask." She went in the house and slammed the door in his face.

Dan was standing by the coffee table looking shell-shocked.

"I didn't mean to be rude, but that guy is a disgrace." Dorie said as she took off her coat.

"There's something here you might find useful." Dan grabbed a book off the table and held it up. *WAS I BORN RUDE?*

"Jack Reilly told me about that," Dorie replied as she went to the front window and pulled down the shades. "We don't need that guy standing on any ladders to get a look in here." She spotted the bags of pillows in the corner. "Oh my," Dorie said, shaking her head as she peeked in the bag. "It's so sad."

Quickly they walked through the house.

"Mrs. Hopkins certainly didn't bring much with her, did she?" Dan asked as they stood in their bedroom.

"No, she didn't."

The phone rang. Dorie reached over to the nightstand and answered it. "Hello."

"Dorie, it's Jack. Are you all right? We saw you drive past with that reporter close behind."

"That guy is so obnoxious! He had the nerve to ask for one of the apology cards. Can you imagine?"

"Regan and I had a brief encounter with him as well that wasn't very pleasant. Listen, I'd like to get a look at Mrs. Hopkins's car as soon as possible."

"Right away, Jack. Can we get rid of that reporter?"

"Legally, he's allowed to be on the street but not on your property. I'll make that clear to him, if I have to. Regan and I will come over now. Why don't you and Dan watch out the window and come out when you see us approaching?"

"If you don't mind, Jack, I think it would be better if Dan stayed in the house. He really doesn't want to be on camera."

"I don't blame him. It won't take four of us to copy down a license plate number. See you in a minute."

Dorie hung up the phone.

"Thanks, Dorie," Dan said, his tone flat.

"It's okay, honey. We'll be right back." She left the room. A moment later she was opening the front door.

I thought we were so lucky when we bought this place, Dan mused. But this house cost someone her life, and now, if that reporter keeps digging, could cost me my job. He was tempted to lie down on the bed and close his eyes. All he wanted to do was hide. I can't, he thought, as he walked across the hall to his daughter's room and peered out the window.

The reporter was standing on the street calling out questions to Dorie, Jack, and Regan as they stepped into the garage and pulled down the door. Then he watched as the reporter turned to the camera and started to speak into his microphone. With his free hand he was gesturing toward the garage.

Dan started to panic. I can't just stand here, Dan thought. I have to help. There must be something in this house that will give a clue as to who Adele Hopkins was. He strode out of the room and headed toward the dining room table to have another look at the cards.

If he'd given in to the temptation to lay down on the bed, he might have discovered one clue without even trying. Right under Adele's pillow.

32

Devon was at his wit's end. First he called his part-time assistant in New York City, only to find out that the prop and scenery truck was parked at a garage on Long Island where it would be safe for the weekend.

"Grant, I need the knives," Devon said. "Floyd Wellington wants to use a real knife for the reading and I would never even consider giving him permission."

"That would be out of the question," Grant agreed.

"I'd like you to go out to the truck and retrieve the knives, then send them up to me on overnight delivery."

"That, too, is out of the question."

"Grant, please!"

"I can't. The streets are flooded, the garage is a long way out on the expressway, and I have a show tonight. Besides which, I'd have to unpack the whole truck to find the knives."

"Grant, this is a desperate situation."

"I'm sure you'll figure something out."

"Please, Grant. I give you work, which you need."

"Work running around town, for which you pay me next to nothing. I'm an actor and you didn't hire me for your show. I could have played the part of the daughter's boyfriend."

"He's twenty-one! You're thirty-one."

"So what. It's the theater. There are no close-ups."

"Goodbye, Grant."

"Goodbye, Devon. Talk to you tomorrow."

Next, Devon tried calling theaters on the Cape. Some of them were still closed for the winter. Others had nothing but information on their recordings that instructed the caller in great detail how to buy tickets for upcoming shows. Devon left a friendly message on two theater answering machines explaining who he was, what he needed, and if anyone could possibly find the time to please call back, he'd be forever grateful.

After he left the second message, hopeful that one of the theaters might be able to help him, one of his mother's favorite sayings came to mind. "Don't count your chickens before they're hatched."

Immediately Devon went out to his car and headed to Provincetown, an artsy community at the tip of Cape Cod. There must be something I can find in one of their unique little shops that looks enough like a knife, he thought.

After an hour and fifteen minutes of driving through the pouring rain, Devon parked his car in a public lot and walked over to Commercial Street. During the summer the street was filled with tourists who strolled, shopped, and dined at the outdoor cafés. Many sat at benches, holding their ice cream cones and people-watching. Right now there were no people to watch; the street was nearly empty.

Devon was cold and wet and near despair as he walked down the block, looking back and forth for a storefront that might suggest a fake knife could be found inside. I don't want to have my palm read, he thought. I don't need a T-shirt. I'm not hungry. Then he saw it. A little shop that had a mishmash of leather, jewelry, costumes, and masks in its window display. Here goes, he thought, as he stepped inside the shop.

The only person inside was a young man with a Mohawk haircut and rings pierced through his nose, ears, and lips. A variety of silver bracelets nearly covered his sleeveless arms. Black jeans, boots, and a leather vest completed the ensemble. "Hey man, can I help you?"

"I hope so," Devon said, trying to sound cheery. "I need a fake knife that looks as real as possible. It should look like a big kitchen knife. I didn't know whether you might have something like that for sale. You certainly have so many interesting items here in your shop," he said with a wave of his hand. "All these costumes and leather goods. It's so marvelous."

The kid stared at him. His dark eyes were piercing.

"I'm a playwright and director," Devon hastened to explain. "I need it for a reading of a play."

"Gotcha. I was just thinking."

"Oh, that's lovely."

"My workshop's in the back. It'll take me a few minutes. Wait here."

"Yes, of course. Thank you." Devon stood at the counter, praying. He soon heard the whirring of a drill coming from the workshop. He must know what he's doing, Devon thought. I hope I hope I hope.

Twenty minutes later, the young man reappeared. "How's this?" he asked, placing his creation on the counter.

Devon looked down at the most beautiful, realistic fake knife he had ever seen. He picked it up. The handle was made of gleaming wood with silver inlets, the blade was shiny but thank God made of rubber. Tears filled his eyes. "This knife is gorgeous. I don't know how I can ever thank you."

"You can pay me," the shopkeeper said with a smile.

"Of course," Devon said, fumbling for his wallet. "You are a very talented young man."

On the drive home, Devon was elated. Floyd was going to love this knife, he was sure. I absolutely cannot wait to show it to him.

A thought occurred to Devon. Why don't I drive over to Floyd's place right now and surprise him with this knife? The whole experience might create a bond between us. We'll have a good laugh, slap each other on the back, tell each other how wonderful we are. Yes, I'll drive to his place right now.

For the next fifteen minutes, Devon wavered. That whole plan might backfire, he thought. Floyd might get angry that I invaded his privacy by showing up on his doorstep.

I'd better not, Devon finally decided.

Floyd Wellington likes to be alone.

33

Mickey McPhee III was feeling a little gloomy. He was rattling around his beautiful home, located in a picturesque town north of Boston, all by himself. His wife was a lawyer and in the middle of a big case. There was no way she could stay home with him on what he referred to as Grandpa Day. His three kids were grown and out of the house. None of them had wanted to join the family business, a sad truth that hurt him deeply. They hadn't even been tempted. As a result, there was no one in the family he could toss ideas around with, no one to discuss campaigns with, no one to truly celebrate with when the firm landed a big account.

No, he'd never re-create the relationship he had with Grandpa.

Mickey had joined McPhee and You fresh out of college, thirty-eight years ago. For the next twenty years he and Grandpa worked side by side. Together they created campaigns, pitched accounts, and shared the highs and lows of their work. Up until the day Grandpa died in his sleep.

Mickey's father, like Mickey's kids, had had no interest in the business.

Sitting in his tasteful den, with its leather couches and book-lined shelves, Mickey gazed out the window. His home was

perched on a hill and had a magnificent view of the sea—which
on sunny days took your breath away. But today the weather was
awful, which contributed to his sense of malaise. If I had at least
been able to go out and play a round of golf, he thought, I'd feel
better. Grandpa loved golf.

He twiddled his thumbs. A magazine he'd meant to read for
work was on his lap, unopened. Impatiently he picked up the
remote control and flicked on the television. A news station was
reporting how dangerous the storm could be if people weren't
careful. Not surprising, Mickey said to himself, changing the
channel, something he did constantly. His wife hated to watch
television with him because he was only interested in the ads.
After he'd sped through about a hundred channels, he flicked
the television off.

It's been a rough year, he thought. The health club we had
just signed up filed for bankruptcy. Our top writer stole from
the poor box. Not good, Mickey thought. Not good at all. I hope
those contracts come in from the department store. I'm anxious to get started on the campaign. Dan Carpenter certainly
sounded excited about the account.

Mickey smiled. Dan had been with the firm a long time and
was a good worker. Maybe I should open up to him more. Maybe
I should make him a trusted confidant. He isn't family, but I
truly believe he has the firm's best interest at heart. As I told
him, he has good judgment. I think he could become a good
friend.

It's lonely at the top, Mickey thought as he picked up his cell
phone. I'll never have a relationship resembling the one I had
with Grandpa, but maybe Dan and I could become better ac-
quaintances. I'll call him now just to say a friendly hello.

He went through his list of contacts, found Dan's cell phone
number, and pressed send. Already Mickey felt better.

34

When Dan's cell phone rang, the sound of blaring trumpets that might signal the arrival of royalty filled the room. His whole body twitched. The apology card he had just picked up off the dining room table went flying out of his hands. Trembling, he reached down, pulled back the Velcro-lined flap of a holster attached to his blue-and-yellow striped belt, and grabbed his phone. One look at the caller ID sent him into orbit. Mickey McPhee. Next to Mickey's name was a playful image of a tiny old-fashioned phone ringing off the hook, an image that suggested the call was sure to be cheery. But the cartoonish phone appeared onscreen every time the phone rang, no matter whether the call was good, bad, or a wrong number.

This call I know is bad, Dan told himself, as he stared at the little phone dancing merrily around the screen. I can't answer it. Mickey must have seen the television news story that jerk outside filed when Dorie, Jack, and Regan disappeared into the garage. The way that reporter was gesturing, he couldn't have been saying nice things. Dan heard the reporter ask Dorie if she was Mrs. Carpenter, but thankfully he didn't ask anything about Adele Hopkins' background. But if Mickey saw the report he'd want to know every detail of what was going on. Every last detail.

Dah dah dah dahhhhh. Dah dah dah dahhhh. "Stop!" Dan shouted angrily to the phone in his hand. Ordinarily he loved the regal sound of the trumpets. The music had once been used in a commercial for margarine that people mistook for butter. *Dah dah dah dahhhhh.* Now it was fraying his nerves, but he was too paranoid to press the silence button, afraid Mickey would sense that Dan was dissing him. He decided to let the phone ring until voice mail kicked in.

Seventeen quick bursts of music later, the trumpets silenced. The cell phone beeped, indicating a missed call, then about thirty seconds later, made a loud chirping sound indicating Mickey had left a message.

Oh my God, Dan thought. What should I do? I'm going to have to listen to what Mickey said, but maybe I'll wait. He was staring at the phone when the front door flew open.

Dorie, Jack, and Regan hurried in out of the rain. Dan put the phone back in his holster, walked over and shook Jack's hand, then gave Regan a hug. "Hello, you two. We appreciate your help more than you know," he said, trying to appear calm.

"We're happy to do whatever we can," Regan answered.

"Did you find anything in the garage?" Dan asked hopefully.

"The car is locked but we know it's a rental. There's a sticker on the license plate," Dorie explained. "As I remember, it's the same car she drove over here that day we met her."

Dan clenched his fists. That fateful day at Fern's diner. He looked from Regan to Jack. "I can imagine what you must think. We realize we should have checked out Adele Hopkins. But we didn't. That reporter would just love to hear about that, I'm sure. I feel so foolish."

"I'm telling you, Dan," Dorie said, "our instincts about Adele were right. If the woman hadn't fallen down the steps we wouldn't be in this situation. She didn't do anything wrong, the poor thing. We just have to find out where any family members might be or a friend who will settle her affairs. We know she was recently divorced, so her ex must be somewhere out there. If we find him, he should be able to tell us who to contact."

"*If* she was telling us the truth," Dan said.

"I believe she was," Dorie said firmly. "Look at her things. Self-help books about being rude and irritable, apology cards. This woman had a lot of guilt. She must have been going through some kind of turmoil."

"Let me call my office," Jack said quickly. "When Regan and I were waiting for you to get here, I called my first assistant and briefed him. I'll give him the license plate number and he'll get in touch with the rental car company. They must have Mrs. Hopkins's driver's license information. We'll start from there."

"Jack, why don't you use the phone in the kitchen?" Dorie suggested. "Sometimes the cell phone reception isn't so great in this house."

"Thanks, Dorie," Jack said as he followed her out of the room.

Dan turned to Regan, his face tight with worry. "Did you notice anything on the seat of the car?"

"There was nothing. She could have things in the trunk, but that is obviously locked too." Regan could tell that Dan was a wreck. "There will be a lot we can do with her driver's license information," she said comfortingly. "Right now we should search the house to see if there's anything else that might be helpful."

Dorie had come back from the kitchen. "You know, Regan," she said, "Dan and I just arrived. At first glance it seems Adele Hopkins didn't bring much with her. There aren't many clothes in the closet. No sign of a computer. No personal papers. I know she was just renting for six months, but the place seems so stark."

"It does," Regan agreed. "But if she just got divorced, she might have had to put her things in storage while she was trying to decide what to do with her life, where to live. I get the impression she used this house as a retreat to escape the world. She only had the house for another month, right?"

"Till the middle of May. But where did she get her mail? Nobody can just disappear off the face of the earth for six months. There's no way to avoid bills and paperwork, no matter how much you'd like to."

"We checked to see if she had a PO box at the Chatwich post office. She didn't. Right now, we should take a closer look around the house. Jack and I were only here for a few minutes this morning."

"I can't believe Adele Hopkins woke up here today," Dorie said. "Her breakfast dishes are still in the sink. It breaks my heart."

Regan nodded. "Why don't we look around?" she said softly.

Dorie raised her hands, then dropped them to her sides. "This is a small three-bedroom beach house, simply furnished. Not a lot of nooks and crannies. A damp basement. I'm afraid there aren't many places to explore."

"Well, let's try. Why don't we start with the master bedroom? I was in there this morning but we certainly didn't conduct a search."

Dorie led Regan down the hall, Dan following.

They looked through the drawers, checked the pockets of all Adele's clothes, and opened up her suitcase. They checked the shelves of the closet and under the bed and found nothing that shed any light on her identity.

Dan got up from the floor and started to lift up the mattress from the foot of the bed.

Regan and Dorie both hurried to help. Together the three of

them lifted it high enough to see that there was nothing underneath. When they eased the mattress back down the quilt and two pillows were rumpled.

They lifted the quilt to reveal perfectly tucked sheets, then placed it back down and fluffed up the pillows.

But Adele's most treasured item had slipped down the opening between the headboard and the bed when Dan started to lift the mattress.

"Good news!" Jack called from the kitchen. "We have an address for Adele Hopkins in Illinois."

The three of them hurried from the room.

35

Reed was walking around his apartment, overwhelmed by a feeling of desperation. Olivia had packed quickly and left for the airport. She'd just called him from the cab, crying, wishing him luck with his meeting. All her kindness only made him feel worse. It was bad enough he was worried that she'd discover what Ellen wrote on the website today. But Olivia knew that Ellen couldn't stand him and that Ellen might embellish a story to make him look even worse. Maybe he could explain his way out of that one, and he was determined to make sure it never happened again. But if Olivia found out that he lied about the meeting, she'd bolt on him for good. She understood business and how tough things were these days for everyone, especially him. Her support never wavered when his deals fell apart after Ellen's first hateful interview was published. They'd discussed different projects he was trying to get off the ground and her suggestions were always helpful. He'd been sneaky for no reason, inventing a meeting that she'd probably want to know all about. It was completely stupid. In the end, Olivia would never stick with a pathetic, lying loser.

He felt as if his whole life was crumbling around him.

What am I going to do to make Ellen stop? What? he asked himself as he walked back and forth in front of his big windows overlooking Boston Harbor. I could go down to the Cape and try and reason with her, but that could easily go wrong. She might write about it on her website and make him look like an even bigger sleaze. If Olivia found out, she might assume he really had been interested in Ellen.

If only I hadn't gotten away with being such a jerk to all those women I dated, he thought. No matter how bad I was, I always got away with it. No one confronted me, except the woman I secretly courted when I was engaged to my wife twenty years ago. She called Sweetsville screaming when she read about his marriage in the newspaper. He and his wife were on their honeymoon and were never coming back. He'd been transferred to a different office. After the honeymoon, the couple went straight to their new home, ten states away. His old boss who had taken the call, found it amusing.

Then, after fifteen years of marriage, his wife found out he was having a fling and filed for divorce. No discussion. No counseling. The only thing he regretted was that his daughter had sided with her mother and didn't want to see him anymore. Every month he sent alimony and child support, and as of September he had to cover the tuition of an expensive private college. For the daughter he hadn't seen in years.

When I met Olivia, it was the first time I'd really fallen in love. She was the first woman I was afraid of losing. Flirting with Ellen the night the restaurant opened meant nothing, I was being my usual self. I never in a million years thought my behavior would come to this. Now anyone in the world can turn on their computer and read about how I met women, my failed restaurant, unreturned phone calls to a hardworking employee, and my cheating heart. I'll never get another deal going. I'll lose Olivia. I could end up on the street.

Reed's heart started beating so fast he thought his chest would explode. With purpose, he headed to the liquor cabinet and poured himself a glass of scotch. He had taken one sip when his cell phone rang. It was his mother. Her timing had always been uncanny.

"Hi, Mom." That first sip of scotch tasted good, he thought.

"Hello, dear. You tried to kiss that girl who has the pillow shop?"

"What?"

"I just heard that from the guy here at the club who is on the internet all the time. I think he likes to taunt me because I won't go out with him. But really, dear, this is embarrassing. He's spreading the word that my son wasn't raised right and doesn't know how to treat women. Every time I see him he asks if I've received any new makeup in the mail. Why don't you talk to that girl and tell her what she's doing isn't ladylike? Write her a letter or something."

"I will."

"Send it today."

"Okay."

"Do you promise?"

"Yes, I promise."

"Good. How's Olivia?"

"Her father is sick. She's on her way to Atlanta."

"You didn't go with her?"

"No."

"Why not?"

"I haven't met her parents yet. She doesn't think this is the time."

"Olivia hasn't met me yet, but if I were sick, I'd expect her to come down to Florida with you. I can't understand why you haven't met each other's parents yet, but that's another story. I think you should be with her in her time of need."

"She didn't want me to go."

"You should have insisted!"

"Mom!" Reed protested. He couldn't tell her that Olivia thought he had a meeting. "Olivia's mother is formal—"

"Well, you two have been together long enough. If she's so wonderful, you should at least be engaged by now. Neither one of you is a kid anymore. You need to settle down and get a job. Why don't you call Sweetsville and see if they'll take you back? You never know, maybe they realize they made a mistake—"

Reed snapped the phone shut and threw it across the room. His head was about to explode. "Call up Sweetsville?" he breathed, his voice trembling. "Sure, Mom. Good idea!" He raced toward the bedroom, scotch in hand, and pulled an over-night bag out of the closet. Before putting the glass of scotch on his dresser, he took a big gulp. It took him three minutes to pack his bag. He zipped it up, downed the rest of the scotch, and called for the car.

Olivia was the only good thing left in his life.

I'm going to do whatever I can to keep her, he thought, tears stinging his eyes. Whatever it takes.

He picked his phone off the floor, strode out of his apartment, and called for the elevator.

What I'd really love to do, he thought, is to hold one of Ellen's precious pillows over her face. Hold it over her face until she smothers.

He smiled and quickly wiped his eyes. Wouldn't that make a great story for the Pillow Talk website?

36

Adele took a final glance in the bathroom mirror, gently touching her swollen nose. I'm sure I broke it when I fell, she thought. It certainly doesn't look like a pug nose anymore.

She stood at the door and took a moment to collect herself, scared, but aware that she couldn't let Floyd know. Bullies thrive on the power they derive from instilling fear in their victims. Something she'd finally come to understand after years of living with one of the biggest bullies on earth. I should have stood up to my ex-husband but I didn't. Now I've got nothing to lose. I'll handle Floyd like I should have handled that wretched excuse of a human being, the biggest mistake of my life, the most rotten—

"Adele! I'm waiting!"

Adele grabbed the handle of the door forcefully and pulled it open. "Don't rush me," she snapped, looking Floyd straight in the eye. She breezed past him and walked back to the living room. "I'm hungry," she said as she sat back down on the couch.

"Hungry?" Floyd roared as he charged back into the living room. "Did I hear you correctly?"

"Yes, you did."

"I'd take you to lunch but people might talk. You're a mess. Come on, we have work to do," he said, reaching for his script.

"Did you eat when you were at rehearsal?"

"No, as a matter of fact I didn't. The others had just come from breakfast. They didn't invite me." He shrugged. "I guess they knew better. But the director didn't even offer me so much as a cup of *coffee*."

"That's a shame. Where is your play being performed?"

"Somewhere called The Castle by the Sea."

"That's not a theater," Adele scoffed.

"*I know that, Adele!* You don't have to tell me. We will be performing under a tent on their vast front lawn."

"When does your show open?"

"Memorial Day," he said, looking down at his script.

What is he going to do with me? Adele wondered. He can't keep me here forever. I'm not going to think about it, she decided. Right now I'm hungry. I only had toast for breakfast. I ache all over and I need to eat something.

"Adele, turn to page—"

"*No!* Don't you have any food here?" Adele demanded. "I'm starving and I feel faint." She leaned back on the couch and started rubbing her head.

Floyd looked up from his script. "We wouldn't want that to happen, now would we? No we wouldn't. I need you to help me learn my lines. You're not much of an actress, but"—he paused, rolled his eyes, and shook his head back and forth—"we weren't all meant for the stage."

I'm acting now, Adele thought. I'm trying to appear confident even though I'm terrified. "Don't you have any food in this house?"

"It's not my house! I arrived late last night. I'm sorry I didn't go shopping, Adele. You're very demanding."

"But I smelled coffee. And you made me tea with milk. Where did that come from?"

Floyd threw the script on the chair. "My director, okay! He arranged with the real estate agent to have someone drop off a few provisions so I could have breakfast. English muffins, juice, coffee, tea bags, milk . . . that's it! They certainly didn't go overboard. I found a rotten tomato in the vegetable bin. I can slice that up for you." He paused. "Would you like an English muffin?"

"I'd like an omelette. With an English muffin on the side."

Floyd looked stunned. "With or without jelly?" he screamed as he paced back and forth, running his fingers through his hair.

"With."

Floyd stopped in his tracks.

"Neither one of us had much food today," Adele said softly. "You need to eat."

"Thanks, Mom," Floyd said sarcastically. Wearily he sat down on a chair. "I suppose I am a bit hungry. Don't expect me to cook anything, though. And I'm not letting you near any sharp utensils. Takeout food is the answer. The cast said the food was good at the diner they went to this morning, but I was only half listening."

"There's a diner down the road from the Castle called Fern's. It's probably where they went."

Floyd's eyes narrowed. "Have you been there?"

"Only once."

"You couldn't have liked it much."

"The food was delicious. But I came to Cape Cod to be alone."

"Why?"

"I was recently divorced and I wanted time to myself to think things through. If you recall, I told you there would be no one waiting at home for me."

"There's no one waiting for me either, Adele. I've had three wives who've all flown the coop."

What a shock, Adele thought. I wonder what shape they're in today.

As if reading her mind, Floyd said, "One of them remarried, one swore off men, and the third is now dead." He stood. "What can I get you at Fern's?"

"An omelette with everything, hold the mushrooms, well done."

"If you hold the mushrooms, then it's not with everything."

"It's easier than listing all the other ingredients."

"What are the other ingredients?"

"I don't know, Floyd!" Adele barked. "Whatever they have. Tomatoes, cheese, peppers, whatever."

Floyd ignored her outburst as he scribbled on his script. "Very well. Anything else?"

"Chicken soup."

Floyd finished scribbling. "I'll study my lines while they prepare the food." He stood. "Back downstairs, my dear. But not for too long this time." He smiled. "When I return we'll eat, then get back to work. I want to have all my lines memorized for the reading tomorrow night."

"What reading?"

"A reading at the Castle. It's a fundraiser disguised as a cocktail party. Too bad I can't invite you."

"I told you," Adele said, her nose in the air, "I came here to be alone."

37

When Regan, Dorie, and Dan hurried into the kitchen, Jack was still on the phone talking to his assistant. "Right," he said. "Uh-huh."

Uh-huh what? Dan wondered frantically.

"Thanks, Keith. Talk to you soon." Jack hung up the phone. "The address on Adele Hopkins's license is an apartment building in Chicago. My office is getting in touch with our contacts out there. They have already determined that no phone is listed at that address. The police will find out if there's an apartment in her name. My guys are running a check on her license now to see what else might turn up."

"These days there are lots of people who only have cell phones," Dan said anxiously. "Just because there isn't a phone at that address doesn't have to be bad news for us, right?

"Not at all," Jack answered. "A lot of people don't bother with landlines anymore. Also, if Hopkins was recently divorced, this could be a temporary apartment and she wouldn't have bothered to get a phone. As long as she used the apartment as her legal residence, we should be in good shape. She'd most likely receive mail there, that kind of thing. Somebody will go over to the building. She might have a family member living there now."

"Wouldn't that be great?" Dan asked excitedly.

Dorie glared at him. "Great for us, Dan, not for them."

"If there's no one living there," Jack continued, "they'll question the doorman, if there is one. They'll talk to the neighbors, that kind of thing."

"Worst-case scenario?" Dan asked, his voice a squeak.

"Worst-case scenario?" Jack repeated. "She moved out and hadn't changed her license yet. Left no forwarding address. No contact numbers on the paperwork for the apartment."

Dan sighed. "Like us. Except we didn't even have any paperwork."

"Let's not dwell on that anymore," Dorie said flatly. "Jack, how long will this take?"

"Running her license is easy. That's done by computer. It's hard to say how long the footwork will take. It really depends on how busy they are right now. They know we wanted the information yesterday, but if they're dealing with more pressing cases, then we'll have to wait a little longer."

"Speaking of computers, I cannot believe there's no computer here. How does anyone survive without a computer these days?" Dorie asked. "I just don't get it. She wasn't that old."

"There could be a lot of explanations," Regan said. "Jack and I have a few other things we want to tell you."

"What?" Dan and Dorie both asked.

Regan looked over at Jack.

"Go ahead," he said.

"Dorie, Jack told you we were planning to go over to Pillow Talk, the store where Adele bought the pillows and the cards. Pippy and Ellen, the two young women who run the shop, remembered Mrs. Hopkins but said she was only in the store a few times and wasn't a talker. They don't know much about her at all. But the GRUDGE pillows they made only for her. She wanted one right away, so they made it overnight. That was in January. A month later she picked up the others. That afternoon they received a GRUDGE pillow in the mail. It was obviously that first one, which I imagine she sent to someone very important to her. It was slashed to ribbons. There was no note. The package was postmarked Long Branch, Massachusetts."

Dorie's hand flew to her mouth. "Slashed?"

"We have it over at the house," Jack said.

"If Adele sent it to someone, she must not have used a return address." Dan said. "How did they know to return it to the shop?"

"The address of the store was on the label of the pillow," Jack explained.

"Long Branch is south of Boston. Do you think this person could have come here, found Mrs. Hopkins, and pushed her down the stairs?" Dorie asked.

"Anything's possible, but it doesn't seem likely," Jack said. "We know she was here this morning—breakfast dishes were in the sink. Fran, Ginny, and Skip all said she loved that rowboat. My parents saw her out rowing in January. Her wallet, keys, and cell phone are not here. My guess is she was going out anyway and decided to check on her boat because of the storm. I doubt someone dragged her to the staircase and threw her down."

"I wonder who Adele sent that pillow to," Dorie said. "They must have been really angry."

Dan pointed to the dining room. "Why did she want to say 'I'm sorry' to so many people?"

Dorie shook her head. "I would never in a million years have guessed how she was feeling. If anything, she seemed sad and a little broken. Not someone who needed to learn how to stop being rude."

"Fran and Ginny thought she was rude," Regan reported.

"Well, those two!" Dorie cried.

"And she wasn't friendly to Skip, who really is a sweet kid."

"I just wish he had the brains to—"

"Dorie," Jack said, "when an accident like that happens, you have to be very careful about moving people in case they've broken their back or have a head injury. He made the right decision. In all these years I've never seen waves that powerful on this beach. It was unbelievable."

Regan turned to Dan and Dorie. "There's one more thing,"

For a brief moment, Dan shut his eyes. No more, he thought. But I guess I don't have a choice.

Regan told them about the e-mail Pippy and Ellen had received from an anonymous woman who complained about a rowing coach named Adele Hopkins whose nose she wanted to break, Pippy's angry response, then the blistering reply back to Pippy.

"A rowing coach who would be one hundred ten years old now?" Dorie asked.

"That's what the e-mail said. None of it is necessarily true or relevant to us. But while we were over at the house waiting for you we sent an e-mail and asked the anonymous person to please write back. She knows from Pippy's e-mail that our Adele Hopkins drowned. If she has a heart she'll give us whatever information she has about where her Adele Hopkins lived and her background."

"She said she wanted to break her nose? I don't think you'll hear back," Dan said, shaking his head.

Regan half smiled. "Jack and I know that doesn't help our chances of receiving a fact-filled reply."

Dan's eyes widened. "Can you imagine if the two Adele Hopkinses were related? Rowing is in the genes. It sounds as if the older Adele Hopkins could have used at least one or two apology cards herself."

"These girls at Pillow Talk have really seen some action," Dorie said. "I read a story in one of the Boston papers—how the original newspaper article about them losing their jobs spread like wildfire once it hit the internet. But the way one of the girls trashed her ex-boss was unbelievable. He must be furious."

Dan's stomach did a flip-flop. He still hadn't checked Mickey McPhee's message.

"From what Ellen said, he was extremely unfair to her," Jack said.

"Yes, but now the girls receive crazy e-mails and a slashed pillow. If I were those two I'd be a little nervous about all the negative feelings their business has stirred up." She looked at Regan. "Anything else you want to tell us?"

Regan smiled. "No."

"Thank God for that."

"Jack," Regan said, "we looked through the master bedroom and didn't find anything helpful. While we're waiting we may as well search the rest of the house to see if there is an address book or paperwork or something else that might make this whole process a little easier."

"Let's do it."

38

Fran and Ginny stood at either end of the large piece of plywood, holding it against the broken window, while Skip hammered it in place. The wind was howling and the rain slapped their slickers.

Ginny shouted to Fran, "When Skip is finished we'll pack a bag and head back to the Reillys'."

Fran nodded. "Um-hmmm. Jack Reilly is a fine fellow. He did some job hanging that plastic for us. Our living room is in good shape."

"Yes, but it's still damp and drafty," Ginny protested, panicked at the thought that their home might be habitable. "We shouldn't stay here until we get the window replaced." She was dying to get back to the middle of all the action. And now the Carpenters had arrived. There's no way I'm sitting home today, she thought. If need be, I'll break another window myself.

When Skip was finished, he stepped down from his ladder.

"Beautiful job, Skip," Ginny exclaimed. "I always liked the look of natural wood. There's something so earthy."

"Super job," Fran agreed.

"Thanks," Skip muttered. He closed the ladder, picked up his toolbox, and carried them over to his truck. "See you later," he called, with a wave of his hand.

Fran and Ginny hurried across the slippery lawn. "Where are you going?"

"I've got other jobs. The Reillys aren't the only people I work for."

"But Skip, we don't want you to leave. And we have to pay you . . ."

"Don't worry about it. I have to check on other houses, which I should have done this morning."

"You're coming back for supper, aren't you?"

Skip opened the door of the truck. "I don't know. I certainly don't want to come back if that reporter hasn't left."

"We have your number," Fern said. "We'll call you. I know Ginny and I are not the kind of gals that you'd normally spend Friday nights with, but please come back for dinner. Plan to stay over with us at the Reillys'."

"Jack Reilly is such a doll," Ginny said.

"Regan is too."

"She's all right," Ginny answered. "What can I tell you? I have a sweet spot for Jack."

"This is a nightmare," Skip said under his breath as he climbed in the truck.

"Don't be so upset!" Ginny blurted, assuming Skip was just referring to Mrs. Hopkins's death. "Mrs. Hopkins fell down all those steps. You said she was bloody. Skip, chances are ninety-nine to one she was dead. Probably more like 99.9999 . . ."

He turned on the truck's engine. "The slim chance that she was still alive will always haunt me."

Ginny and Fran watched him back out, then disappear down the road.

"Such a shame," Ginny said.

"Yup," Fran agreed, taking a look in the other direction. "That darn reporter is still here. I hope he leaves soon. Skip needs to be with us tonight."

They went back in the house. Ginny pulled a big suitcase out of the closet in the hallway. "We may as well pack enough clothes so we don't have to go running back and forth."

"Good thinking."

The phone rang. Fran hurried into the kitchen to answer. "Hello . . . Hi, Margie . . . Yes, a lot of excitement on our block today . . . What? . . . You don't say . . . We hadn't heard that, we had to have our window boarded up, a branch crashed through . . . What a mess . . . Thanks, we'll let you know." She hung up.

"What?" Ginny demanded. "What?"

"Margie heard on the news that Adele Hopkins must have been very unhappy. The police found stacks of apology cards on her dining room table."

"Apology cards?" Ginny repeated, her face indignant. "How about a thank-you note for that lovely homemade pie we hand-delivered? Fran, let me tell you know something, I knew we were making a mistake by going with Skip to House Junction. We couldn't even listen to the radio!"

"That was the right thing to do," Fran said. "Skip is suffering. Besides, we needed to get this place boarded up."

"I understand. But I don't want to miss out on another thing. Let's go now. Regan and Jack must have loads to tell us, I can feel it in my bones." She ran to the bathroom, where she'd hung up their coats.

"What about packing the suitcase?" Fran asked.

"There's plenty of time for that later," Ginny said as she ran past her older sister toward the front door. "Come on, Fran! I want to get a look at those apology cards. Maybe one of them has our names on it!"

39

Ah, here it is," Floyd said, turning his car into Fern's parking lot. Quaint little place, I suppose, he thought.

Inside the diner, a woman hurried over as he came through the door. "Can I help you?"

Floyd, the script under his arm, smiled his most charming smile. "I'd like to order some food to go."

"Follow me and we'll get you taken care of."

Floyd did as he was told.

"I'm Fern," the woman said, turning around when they reached the counter. "Have a seat."

"Fern of Fern's?"

"Yes."

"Floyd Wellington. Lovely to meet you. I've heard your food is delectable."

Fern smiled, then eyed the script. *Grandpa, Go Home.* "Oh, of course. You're in the play down at the Castle."

"Last I heard," Floyd joked.

"Sorry, I didn't realize it was you. I know you were in a great movie but I never saw it."

"No great loss, my dear."

"The rest of the cast was in here this morning."

"That's why I'm here now. Your place is highly recommended."

Oh, no, Fern thought. That means Devon will be back. "My waitress will take your order."

A young girl, pen poised, smiled at him. "Ready?"

"Yes, darling. I'd like a cheeseburger with fries; an omelette with the works, hold the mushrooms, well done; one chicken soup; and a large fruit salad."

"Toast for the omelette?"

"No. An English muffin with jelly."

"What kind?"

"No preference."

"Anything else?"

"That's enough, isn't it?" he laughed. "I'm stocking up for the evening so I won't have to leave the house again in this dreadful weather."

The girl smiled and disappeared into the kitchen.

Floyd looked down at his script and turned the page. It's a little noisy in here with that television on, he thought. I must focus.

Fern returned. "All squared away?"

He looked up. "I placed my order. Thank you."

"How's it going over there at the Castle?"

"So far, so good."

"You're all living there together?"

Floyd made a face. "Noooooo. No. No no no no no." He then pointed his finger to his head and pretended to pull an imaginary trigger.

Fern laughed. "That would be a no."

"I'm too old to live in a dormitory, darling. The production company rented a house for me."

He probably can't take Devon either, Fern thought. "If I were you, I'd feel the same way," she said. "I live alone. When I leave here, where I'm on the go and with people all day, it's a pleasure to just go home and be by myself. There's nothing like peace and quiet."

Floyd reached up and touched her arm for just a moment. "Surely you must have someone in your life," he said solicitously.

"Not for a while, I haven't," she laughed. "It's okay."

"I can tell you're the type of person who has so much to give another human being. Besides, all work and no play is no fun at all. Are you coming to our reading tomorrow night?"

"Your director invited me. I'll have to see."

"You'll enjoy it," Floyd promised. "And I wouldn't just say that." He leaned toward her and whispered conspiratorially, "The play is good, even though the man directing it makes me cuckoo."

Fern laughed heartily. "He was in here this morning. He makes me cuckoo too." She looked up at the television screen. The announcer had just mentioned Adele Hopkins's name. She shook her head. "I don't know whether you heard, but a woman's body was swept out to sea on the beach this morning not far from the Castle."

"I heard," Floyd said, turning his face to the television. "It is a tragedy." With a duly pained expression he listened to the report.

"On the dining room table of the house Adele Hopkins was renting were stacks of apology cards she had not yet addressed."

Floyd looked at Fern and raised his eyebrows. "Apology cards?"

"Yes."

"Did you know her?"

"No. I'm told she was in here once." Fern's head turned reflexively at the sound of the front door opening. At the same moment the young waitress reappeared from the kitchen with three bags of food. "All set!" she said with a smile.

"Wonderful!"

Fern started to move down the counter. "Nice to meet you, Floyd. Thanks for coming in."

"Return the favor by coming to our reading tomorrow night."

"I promise I'll try."

Floyd paid with cash and got up just as Fern was greeting a young man who took a seat three stools down.

"Skip, there's no one in the other room. Do you want to take a table back there by the window? I'll sit with you."

"Thanks, Fern."

That young man doesn't look too happy, Floyd thought as they nodded to each other in passing. But Floyd didn't give the young man's state of mind another thought.

Apology cards were on his mind as he went out the door. He laughed out loud as he got into the car. I can't wait to tell her that the whole world knows how very, very sorry she is.

One thing is clear, he thought as he pulled out of the parking lot. She's not as tough as she pretends to be. I knew that all along.

She's a lousy actress but at least she'll help me learn my lines.

Then what?

Sweat broke out on his forehead. He refused to think about that now. He had to learn his lines.

40

Kit breathed a sigh of relief as she crossed the Sagamore Bridge onto Cape Cod. The traffic from Boston had been lousy. Speed limits had been lowered because of the slick roads. Cars passing through puddles sprayed water on other motorists' windshields. *I probably should have just gone home,* she mused. *Oh well. I'm almost there.*

As she rode along Route 6, the main highway on the Cape, more ominous clouds moved in overhead and the sky darkened. *There's no sign of this storm letting up,* Kit thought. Twenty-five minutes later the song Kit was enjoying was interrupted by the bossy female voice of the GPS. "Exit to the right in one mile." Kit put on her right blinker and steered into the exit lane. She was in the market for a new car but hadn't yet decided on a make or model. But one thing she had decided was that her next GPS had to sound a lot friendlier. If you missed a turn, this woman got nasty. "Exit to the right," she now ordered. "Exit to the right."

Kit started to turn off the highway just as her windshield wipers made a loud groaning noise, as though the effort to keep the windshield clear of water was suddenly too much. But they kept working, albeit more slowly, sounding as though they were pushing a boulder uphill. Please, no, Kit thought as she reached the end of the exit ramp and turned left. Keep going, she prayed as the wipers grew more and more sluggish.

At Route 5A Kit turned right and pressed the navigation button on her dashboard. Five miles to go. Her heart was racing as she leaned forward, straining to see through the increasingly blurry windshield. This is too dangerous, she decided. A little gas station was just ahead. Kit put on her blinker and slowed down as the wipers emitted a final exhausted groan. Carefully, she turned into the driveway, which ended as soon as it began.

Kit rolled down her window, stuck her head out, and inched forward, stopping in front of a one-door garage. She rolled up the window, and shut off the car. Rain was pelting her windshield. The wipers were sticking straight up. Kit glanced at her surroundings. A lone set of gas pumps looked forlorn. The garage door was shut, but at least the small office appeared to be open. She sighed, then almost laughed, suddenly reminded of the running gag she had with Regan when things like this happened. One would call the other and start the conversation by saying, "Just when you thought things couldn't get any worse . . ."

It could be worse, Kit thought. At least I'm not out on the highway. She opened her door, stepped out onto the pavement, and hurried inside a glass door to a room no bigger than a cubicle. The register was to the right, on a counter crammed with boxes of candy, gum, and breath mints. A wide assortment of car air fresheners was hanging on the wall to the left. Straight ahead was a lone folding chair. Behind the counter was a doorway to the garage. Kit could see legs sticking out from under a car that was slightly raised.

"Hello," she called, trying to sound cheery.

"Be with you in a minute or two," a man called back, his tone a touch too casual.

"Okay," Kit answered. Five minutes later she sat on the plastic folding chair and crossed her legs. Something tells me this is going to take awhile, she thought, her spirits sinking. She looked over at the rows and rows of air fresheners. A moment later her nose began to itch.

41

In downtown Chicago, a fortyish man hurried through the rotating door of a luxury apartment building. Inside the handsomely appointed lobby, a young concierge wearing a name tag was seated at a large desk.

The man pulled out his badge. "My name is Detective Lopez. If you don't mind, I'd like to ask you a few questions."

"Of course."

"George is your name?"

"Yes."

"Can you tell me if a woman named Adele Hopkins has an apartment in this building?"

"Oh sure, Mrs. Hopkins. She moved in last year but hasn't been here for a long time."

"Is there anyone else living in her apartment?"

"No."

"Is the manager here now?"

"He left for the weekend."

"Do you know if Adele Hopkins gets mail delivered to this address?"

"Yes. A guy who works the overnight shift forwards Mrs. Hopkins her mail every two weeks. She pays him pretty well, I gather. Jessie gets friendlier with the tenants than some-body like me who works during the day. When people come in late, it's quiet, if they've had a few pops, they start chatting. You know what I'm saying?"

Detective Lopez nodded.

"I don't mean that that was the case with Mrs. Hopkins, not at all. But Jessie says that sometimes in the middle of the night he sees some crazy stuff." George paused. A troubled expres-sion came over his face. "Did something happen to her?"

"Yes," Lopez said quietly. "She was living on Cape Cod. They're in the middle of a bad storm right now. She was on the beach this morning and was washed out to sea."

George shook his head, and leaned back in his chair. "Oh, no! That's a shame. Jessie is going to feel really bad."

"Do you have his number?"

The concierge nodded, pulled open a drawer, and reached for a binder. A minute later he held out a piece of paper with Jes-sie's full name, address, cell number, and home phone, neatly written. "He'll be in tonight at eight."

Lopez looked at the address. "He lives pretty far away."

"He got engaged, bought a great house his fiancée loves, and now it takes him two hours to get to work! I tell him he's crazy. But he works a twelve-hour shift, three days a week, so he doesn't mind."

"Do you know if he has a key to Mrs. Hopkins's apartment?"

"Yes he does. He checks for leaks, if her mailbox gets full he brings the mail upstairs, that kind of thing."

"Does the management company have a key to her apart-ment?"

"No, only Jessie." George lowered his voice. "Jessie told me her ex-husband is pretty bad. When she moved in last year she didn't leave a key with the management. She was afraid her ex would sweet-talk his way into getting into the apartment when she was out." George rubbed his fingers together. "He has a lot of dough. They were going through a nasty divorce. That guy was supposedly really controlling. She was afraid to leave any important papers around, you know what I'm saying?"

Lopez nodded. He pulled out his cell phone and dialed Jessie's home number. A machine picked up. Then he dialed Jessie's cell phone and got his voice mail. The detective left a message for Jessie to call him as soon as possible.

George smiled and waved his hand. "That guy never picks up his phone. He sleeps weird hours so he always has his phones shut off."

"What does his fiancée think about that?" Lopez asked.

George rolled his eyes. "He has another cell phone that no one has the number to, except his fiancée. I'm telling you, I think Mrs. Hopkins must have been paying him way too much money."

42

The search of the Carpenters' home proved fruitless. Regan, Jack, Dorie, and Dan couldn't find a thing that shed any light on Adele Hopkins's life. They were all coming up the stairs from the basement when the doorbell rang.

"Who's that?" Dan asked. "That reporter wouldn't have the nerve, would he?"

Regan was the first one up the steps. She opened the door, hurried into the living room, and looked out the window to the front porch. "It's Fran and Ginny."

"What do they want?" Dan asked anxiously.

"They're our house guests for the weekend," Jack answered, his tone wry.

Ginny spotted Regan at the window and held up a FedEx box. "This is for you," she shouted, pointing back and forth between the package and Regan.

Regan acknowledged Ginny by waving her hand in the air, then moved away from the window. "She's delivering a FedEx package for me."

"A FedEx package?" Jack asked. "We're only here for the weekend."

"I have no idea what it might be," Regan answered.

The doorbell rang again.

"Let's keep things vague with these two," Dan pleaded. "No specific answers to questions about Mrs. Hopkins . . ."

Dorie opened the door. "Well, hello, ladies."

"Hello, Dorie," Ginny cried as she stepped inside, Fran in her wake. "My goodness, is it wet outside or what? Hello, Dan."

Dan greeted the two sisters. "Good to see you," he lied.

"Regan," Ginny said, waving the box triumphantly. "Fran and I came back to the house and rang the bell. The door's locked. We turn around and see the FedEx truck rumbling down the road. Good thing we were there, right? The reporter outside was trying to find out who it was for, the name of the sender, but believe me, I kept my mouth zipped," she said, pretending to zip her mouth as she relinquished the package. "It's from your mother." She turned to Dorie and Dan. "Our house is so damp and drafty you wouldn't believe it. Right, Fran?"

"I sneeze just thinking about the conditions in our living room. Brrrr."

"A branch went through our front window this morning," Ginny continued. "Skip put up a piece of plywood but until we get that window replaced, it's going to be very unpleasant. The chill is running right through me as I speak. Luckily we can stay with Jack and Regan."

Regan nodded. "I appreciate your taking such good care of this," she began, indicating the box in her hands.

"Aren't you going to open it?" Ginny asked.

"I'll wait until Jack and I go back to the house in a few minutes. Sorry about the locked door. We thought Skip would be coming back with you."

"He took off for parts unknown," Ginny reported.

"Oh boy," Regan said as she turned to Jack. "Would you give

Ginny the key so she and Fran can go over and take off their wet coats and shoes and warm up? I hate to see them so chilled."

"We're fine," Ginny insisted. "There's no rush. It's nice to say hello to Dorie and Dan." She turned to them again. "I'm sorry about Mrs. Hopkins. We didn't get the chance to know her. Have you reached her family?"

"Almost," Dan answered.

"Skip's a wreck. He feels just terrible. What can you do, right? These things happen."

"They do," Dan agreed.

"Fran and I were just told by a friend about all the apology cards Mrs. Hopkins left behind. Do you mind if we take a look at one? I see an occasional 'I'm sorry' card on the rack at the drug-store, but I've never heard of buying them in bulk."

A brief, awkward silence followed. "They're just like any other cards," Regan said.

Ginny eyed the dining room table. "Can we just take a peek?" she asked.

"Sure," Dorie answered quickly. "She hadn't written anything inside them yet, so it's not quite as personal."

"She hadn't?" Ginny asked, sounding disappointed, as she and Fran followed Dorie over to the table.

"No."

"Who was she planning to send them to?"

"We don't know."

"Wasn't there a list of names or anything like that? . . . Oh look, here's one." Ginny picked a piece of paper off the table. "Fran, look at this. They're all first names."

Fran squinted. "They sure are. I don't see Fran or Ginny on there, do you?"

"No," Ginny answered. "Dorie, we brought over a pie for Mrs. Hopkins. She didn't invite us in the door, and she never thanked us. She would barely wave hello when she drove by our house."

"I'm sorry about that."

"It's not your fault. You can only find out so much about a person when you rent them your home."

"Only so much," Fran agreed. "You can't find out what's in their heart, that's for sure. You can't predict that they'll be a little rude to the neighbors."

Thank God we put the self-help books out of sight, Regan thought.

Ginny sighed. "Fran, what do you say? Let's go next door. I'd like to have a nice hot cup of tea. Jack, you'll be back soon?"

"Yes. We'll be right there."

Ginny turned, spotted the bags of pillows in the corner, and investigated. "GRUDGE ME, GRUDGE ME NOT?"

"Those belonged to Mrs. Hopkins as well," Dorie explained.

Ginny looked at Fran. "To think she never gave us the time of day."

Fran shrugged. "Her loss."

"Let's go."

As soon as the sisters were out the door, the phone rang. It was Detective Lopez from Chicago.

43

After ten minutes of waiting in the unheated, overly air-freshened room, it occurred to Kit that maybe she should check if the mechanic was still breathing. She got up from the uncomfortable, uneven chair, and stepped over to the counter. The sudden loud noise of a tool rapping against metal reassured her that the man under the car was still of this earth. Nothing like someone who can focus on a job without letting anything disturb them, Kit thought. But what would he do if a customer wanted gas? He didn't even ask why I'm here.

The rapping went on for at least thirty seconds. When it stopped, Kit didn't hesitate. "Excuse me!" she called in a loud voice.

"Yes?"

"I was just wondering if you were going to be tied up for much longer."

"I'm not tied up."

"What I meant was—"

"I know what you meant."

"Oh, okay," Kit said with a very slight laugh, then decided to get right to the point. "My windshield wipers stopped working. I can't drive in this weather. Do you know how long it might take for you to fix them?"

"Depends on what caused the problem." A man rolled out from under the car, hoisted himself up and came out to the office. He appeared to be in his fifties, was thin and wiry, with slicked-back brown hair and a mustache. "I promised I'd fix this car today and it's taking longer than I expected," he said. "I'll get to yours just as soon as I'm done."

"It won't be too late?"

"Nah. I should be finished with the jalopy I'm working on in no time. Besides, this is my business. I'm on my own schedule."

That's for sure, Kit thought. "Is there a place nearby where I can get a cup of coffee? I'll give you my keys. Perhaps you could call my cell after you've had a chance to look at my car."

"Sounds like a plan. There's a coffee shop just up the road a piece," he said, pointing in the direction Kit had been heading. "You're going to walk in this rain?"

"I'll be fine. This raincoat is warm and I have a big umbrella." She put her keys on the counter, then wrote her cell phone number on her business card. "Here," she said. "Do you have a card?"

"I ran out. New ones should be in next week."

"What's your name and number in case I have to call you?"

"Nathaniel Boone," he muttered, then clearly recited his number for Kit as she wrote it down on one of her own business cards.

"Thank you, Daniel. I haven't had lunch—"

"My name is *NATHANIEL* not Daniel. Everybody gets that mixed up. I still don't know what my parents were thinking. I've spent my whole life correcting people. You don't know how annoying it gets."

"Sorry, Nathaniel."

"I forgive you." He turned and went back to work.

Tip for Nathaniel, Kit thought. Never run out of business cards. She turned up the collar of her raincoat, hurried out to the car, and popped open the trunk. As fast as she could, she changed to her sneakers, grabbed an umbrella, opened it, shut the trunk, and started walking. She soon realized that Route 5A was not meant for pedestrians. Should I call Regan? she thought, as she did her best to avoid puddles. I don't want to bother her, but she'll wonder where I am. I'll call her when I get to the coffee shop, she decided.

Kit ambled along for fifteen minutes, past woods and houses, trying not to think about how miserable she was. Nathaniel Boone has no sense of time or distance, she realized as the road curved and the next stretch didn't show any promise of commercial zoning. What's his idea of "up a piece"? She contemplated turning back, then decided against it. I'll call a cab from the coffee shop to bring me back to the gas station. It can't be that much farther. Ten minutes later, her feet soaked, her coat drenched, her umbrella blown inside out, she spotted a storefront in the distance, set back from the road.

A sign finally came into view. PILLOW TALK. Is this the store Regan was talking about? Kit wondered. The store where the woman who died bought those pillows? Doesn't matter if it is or it isn't, I'm going in. I have to get out of this rain.

44

Adele was back in the basement, bound to the same chair as before, the ropes tight around her hands and feet. The radio was once again blasting music that for Adele was akin to nails on a blackboard. What's going to happen to me? She wondered. Floyd is insane. Is he capable of killing me? He must be. What else can he do with me? He can't let me go. Adele pondered a possibility. What if I try to convince him that I won't tell anyone anything if he gives me my freedom? Hey, it's been fun, what an exciting actor you are, I know you were just playing around.

No, it won't work, Adele realized in an instant. He's crazy but functional. He obviously knows what it takes to appear sane in public, and he certainly doesn't want to go to jail. Has he ever been in jail?

She could hear the front door opening and the floor creaking above her. No ringing of the doorbell a hundred times? What a surprise. I guess he doesn't want lunch to get cold.

"I'm SORRRRY," Floyd sang as he thundered down the stops. "So SORRRYYYYY." His laugh was maniacal. "Adele, you must have been a very bad girl."

I wish I'd never set foot in that pillow shop, Adele thought. I sent that first pillow with a heartfelt note and received no response. That's why I never sent the others. And those cards were a stupid idea. I should have thrown them out.

Floyd hopped like a bunny over to her chair.

He's unraveling before my eyes, Adele decided. This might be over faster than I expected.

"I'm sorrrrrry!" Quickly he untied the ropes. *"Lunch is served!"*

Adele slowly pushed herself up from the chair, her body stiff and achy. It was hard for her to believe that this morning she'd been feeling fit, and was looking forward to getting back out on the water in her boat once the storm ended.

"Your chicken soup is going to be cold, Adele. Cold and filmy. *Hurry up!*"

"This house must have a microwave," Adele replied as she walked toward the steps.

"What a waste of time! Move, move, move. We've got work to do."

Upstairs, he instructed Adele to sit on the couch in her same old spot. Bags of food were already on the coffee table as well as two bottles of water. Floyd sat on the floor across from her, located the bag with his foil-wrapped cheeseburger, and quickly tore it open. He whistled as he prepared his burger for consumption, then attacked it with a vengeance.

Adele watched him as she daintily cut her omelette with a plastic knife and fork, and started to eat. The omelette tasted delicious, just as it had the one time she'd been to Fern's. Adele remembered back to that day. The young waitress had been so sweet. It was her third day of work and she was nervous, trying so hard to get everything just right. Naturally she made a few mistakes, like not refilling the coffee cup in a timely fashion, but it was to be expected. What bothered Adele was when the waitress brought her change back to the table and started asking personal questions. She meant to be friendly, but it was one of the reasons Adele never went back. The main reason was that Adele loved sitting at the Carpenters' kitchen table in the early morning, sipping coffee, and looking out on Cape Cod Bay, feeling more at peace than she had in years. And thanks to that house with the view, Adele thought, here I sit.

"*Adele!*" Floyd yelled, licking his fingers. "Where were you just now?"

"Nowhere."

"I don't believe you. Were you thinking about all the people you were going to send apology cards to?" he asked as he opened a plastic container of fruit salad.

"No."

Floyd popped a grape into his mouth. "I want to hear about every last one of them."

"You need to learn your lines."

"Oh I do, do I?"

"Yes. That's my job. Help you learn your lines."

"Your *job?* How interesting. Are you trying out a different psychological approach on wacky Floyd?" Booming laughter filled the room. "That's so funny. I can promise you, *Adele*. It won't work."

"I wasn't trying anything," Adele replied. "You're going to look like a big idiot if you don't learn your lines."

"Tomorrow night is a reading, my dear. It's only one scene. I do intend to be off book so I can wave that big shiny knife in the air just like I do in rehearsal with you and not worry about looking at my script. It will be so much more thrilling for me. I get bored if I don't take risks onstage. I could tell the director really didn't like the idea when I mentioned it earlier today. Just this once I'd like to try it. You're not afraid that Floyd is going to let that big sharp knife go flying into your throat when we rehearse, are you?"

"Not at all," Adele answered, her tone disgusted. "The director doesn't like the idea of you using a real knife?"

"No. They're never used onstage. Only prop knives." Floyd wrinkled his nose. "Toooo dangerous."

The director won't let him use a real knife, Adele thought. How could he? He has to see how volatile Floyd is. Maybe if I can convince Floyd that an actor of his stature should always use a real knife, he'll believe it. I'll try to get him worked up. With any luck, he'll snap tomorrow night and act like a raving lunatic if he's not allowed to use his knife. He'll be exposed as the mad man he really is. It's my only hope. I don't know. It's worth a shot. I want to get out of here. If I do, I will send those cards. Ten years too late, but I'll send them. I never said good-bye to those kids who meant the world to me. And I'll Express Mail the self-help book about being rude to my ex. He's the one who needs it, not me. He was born into too much money and he was born rude. I'm so mad at myself for letting him make me feel as if I were the problem. Well, here goes nothing.

Adele looked Floyd in the eye. "That director doesn't sound very adventurous."

"Unfortunately he's not."

She frowned, "You told me I'm no actress. But if I were on-stage, I'd feel childish using a fake knife."

"Childish?"

"Yes. I'd feel like I was playing a game of cops and robbers." She lifted her thumb and pointed her index finger—"Bang, bang, Floyd. Let's get back to learning your lines."

45

Regan, Dorie, and Dan were sitting at the Carpenters' kitchen table as Jack spoke on the phone to a detective from Chicago who had preliminary information about Adele Hopkins.

Dan was still reeling over the painfully close call with Ginny and Fran. They never would have left if they'd still been inside the house when the phone rang. Also weighing on Dan's mind was the fact that he hadn't even listened to Mickey McPhee's message yet. The longer he waited, the worse he felt. But he was glued to his seat, focused on Jack's half of the conversation. So far it sounded somewhat positive.

Finally the call was wrapping up. Jack was checking to make sure the detective had his cell number and the number of the Reillys' home. "Yes, that's my parents' house, which is right next to where I am—the house Adele Hopkins rented. I'll be at my parents' place from now on."

Dan's eyes bugged out. "What if this guy calls and Fran or Ginny answers?" he whispered to Regan. "Then what?"

"Dan!" Dorie whispered. "Regan and Jack aren't going to sleep here."

"They can if they want to."

"Relax!"

Finally Jack hung up the phone.

"Well?" Dan asked, his voice a croak.

"It's Hopkins's apartment, which I'm sure you gather," Jack said, then relayed the rest of the information. "The concierge who forwards her mail is due at work tonight at nine p.m. Eastern Time. Lopez hopes to speak to him before then, but if not, he'll talk to him at nine. After that I can't imagine we'll have too many more problems figuring out whom to contact."

They all were quiet for a moment.

Dorie's face was solemn. "Adele Hopkins had a horrible ex-husband, no children, no family who visited. What if there isn't anybody to call?"

"There must be someone!" Dan said quickly. "There has to be."

"Dan, you're getting on my nerves."

"But what do we do with her car?"

"We'll bring it back to the rental company. Is that so hard?"

"No use speculating," Regan said. "Remember, we don't even have her cell phone. She might have a lot of friends who were very close to her. Later tonight, we'll know more."

Jack's fingers rapped the countertop. "Okay then. Regan, shall we go next door and join our houseguests?"

Regan stood and smiled at the Carpenters. "You two are most welcome to join us."

Dan shook his head back and forth, staring straight ahead.

"What a surprise, Dan," Regan said lightly. "I understand those Brewer women are very good cooks. They said they'd make dinner."

"They'll just ask and ask and ask about Hopkins," Dan answered. "It's not strange if you two don't know certain answers. It's really strange if we don't."

"If you change your mind . . ." Jack began as he walked over and put his hand on Regan's shoulder.

"We won't," Dan assured him. "But we will see you later, right? Would you mind coming back after you talk to Lopez?"

"Sure. We'll just have to figure some excuse to get out of the house." Jack laughed. "We'll see you later."

The Carpenters walked them to the door, then Dorie moved toward the window and watched as the twosome crossed the lawn together, Jack's arm protectively around Regan. "We're so lucky to have them helping us. I don't know what we would have done if they weren't here." She turned around. "Dan? Dan, where are you?"

His voice came from down the hall. "I have to check my messages, then call my boss right now, while I have the courage," he said. A door slammed shut.

Dorie shook her head. She walked into the kitchen and sat back down at the table. This house feels so empty, she thought. Empty and desolate. Tears stung her eyes. Mrs. Hopkins had planned to enjoy sitting at this table and looking out on the water. I hope she did. It's funny, Dorie thought wistfully. I feel as if in some way she's still here. Her spirit hasn't left us yet. That's how so many people feel right after someone they love dies.

Moments passed. Adele Hopkins wasn't someone I loved, Dorie thought as a tear rolled down her cheek. I barely knew her.

So why do I feel this way?

46

Pippy had been at her desk in the back room of Pillow Talk doing paperwork, going through mail, and answering the phone, while Ellen had handled the light but steady flow of customers.

The phone rang while Pippy was examining a nail she'd just broken on her left hand. She reached for the phone. "Hello. Pillow Talk."

"May I speak to Miss Pippy Huegel, please?" a man with a distinguished British accent inquired.

"This is Pippy."

Silence.

"Hello?"

"How soon they forget," the caller said sadly, now sounding like a born and bred Bostonian.

"Roger!" Pippy cried. "How are you? How was your trip? It seems like you've been gone for ages."

"You live in my house, you become a star, and you never mention your wonderful cousin in all those interviews."

"Yes I do!" Pippy protested, starting to laugh. "And I'm not a star."

"When do you mention me?"

"Today, as a matter of fact. A newspaper reporter called to

set up an interview. We're not very busy with customers and the reporter had time, so I spoke to her right away."

"Um-hmmm. What did you say?" Roger asked, amusement in his voice.

"The reporter asked what it was like to work and live with my best friend. I said it was great and thanks to my cousin, *Roger Huegel,* we didn't have to worry about a place to live when we started the business. He lent us his wonderful cottage on the Cape, blah blah blah."

"I'll believe it when I see it. What newspaper?"

"I wrote the name down here somewhere . . . it's a local paper in California."

"California? I live in Boston! None of my friends will see it."

"We'll send them copies and they can read it online."

"Okay, pal," he said with a chuckle. "How are you?"

"Good. Other than the fact Ellen and I better get going and find a new place to live. Summer is almost here."

"That's right. Cousin Rodge can't wait to get down to the Cape and enjoy himself. What about the lease on your shop? Isn't that up for renewal?"

"Did we luck out on that one! The owner went to Florida, fell in love, and never came back. He renewed with us over the phone for another six months. Same price."

"Ain't love grand?"

"I wouldn't know."

"You're working too hard. Listen, I just got back last night. I have to run to a meeting, but I wanted to say hello and see how the house is holding up in this weather."

"When we left this morning everything was fine."

"Let me know if something lovely happens like the basement floods or . . ."

"Are you worried about that?"

"No, but let's put it this way. If you and Ellen weren't living there, I'd definitely have someone check the house. Even if it cost me a few bucks."

Pippy laughed. "I'll go over there right now."

"Pippy, don't—"

"It's two blocks away. With all you've done for us . . ."

"That's what I like to hear." He laughed. "Keep going."

"We could never—"

"I'm kidding, Pippy. Let me know if there are any problems. I'll get them taken care of."

When Pippy hung up the phone, she smiled. She was looking forward to seeing Roger. It would be fun to have him around this summer. She got up, grabbed her coat, purse, and umbrella, and went out to the front. Ellen was by the door talking to a woman who was drenched from head to toe.

"Really? You're a friend of Regan and Jack's?"

Pippy hurried over and met Kit.

"I don't want to cause a puddle in your store," Kit said with a laugh. "My car is being fixed down the road. The mechanic told me there was a coffee shop up this way, so I started walking and walking . . ."

"Nathaniel Boone?" Ellen asked.

"Yes!"

"A good mechanic, but out of his mind!" Ellen said. "Kit, take off your coat. Have a cup of coffee. There's a table over there. You can sit and call Regan—"

"I hate to interrupt," Pippy said quickly. "Ellen, I'll be right back. Roger called. I think he's worried the basement might flood so I'll run home for a minute and check."

"We'll be here," Ellen said as she helped Kit off with her coat.

Outside, the skies were dark. In a moment Pippy was in her

car and on her way. She barely noticed the car on the side road across the street, waiting to turn onto 5A. When Pippy turned right, the car's left blinker started flashing. The driver accelerated in time to fall in line behind Pippy's car, not too close for comfort, but not in danger of losing her.

47

Mickey McPhee opened his eyes. I must have dozed off, he thought. The den was getting dark. What was I doing? Oh yes. I'd called Dan Carpenter and I was waiting for him to call back. Mickey glanced at his phone. No calls.

Poor me, Mickey lamented. Here I sit, all alone, cranky after my nap. He picked up the remote and turned on the television, quickly changing stations, stopping only when the sight of an overly dramatic reporter speaking into his microphone attracted his interest. The newsman was standing on a little street, the caption at the bottom of the screen read *Chatwich*.

". . . the tragic drowning victim, Adele Hopkins, was a rowing enthusiast who lived alone. The sea had been her friend, then became her enemy. She rented the home behind me, from Daniel and Doreen Carpenter of Boston."

"What?" Mickey cried. "Dan never mentioned he rented out his house on the Cape. I wonder why."

". . . Unfortunately, the Carpenters are not anxious to speak to the media at this time."

Mickey's phone rang. He checked the caller ID, then swiftly answered. "Hello, Dan!"

"Hello, Mickey, how are you on this wonderful company holiday?"

"How are *you?* I just heard your name on television. What's going on?"

"Oh you heard," Dan said, sounding grave.

"Yes I did. What happened? I didn't know you were renting your house. You never breathed a word to me about it."

"We thought it would be nice to rent our home during the winter months to a woman who needed a place to heal from a bad marriage."

"Dan, what happened to her?"

"It's a sad story, Mickey," Dan answered. A most abbreviated version of the day's events followed.

"You rented your house to a recently divorced sixty-year-old woman who loved to row, but she drowned? That's it?"

"What else can one say at a time like this?"

"Does she have children?"

"No."

"Relatives?"

"We're in the process of contacting them."

"Dan, they might need our help! We should do something for them. Or else we can make a donation to Mrs. Hopkins's favorite charity in her memory. What was her favorite charity?"

"I don't know, sir."

"Find out. I've made a decision. McPhee and You will establish a memorial fund in Hopkins's . . . what's her first name?"

"Adele."

"We'll establish a memorial fund in Adele Hopkins's name. McPhee and You has had some bad breaks this year. It's high time we did some good and then let people know about it! This is the perfect opportunity. I'm sure you agree. . . . Hello . . . Dan . . . are you there?"

48

Welcome back!" Ginny called out from the kitchen as Regan and Jack walked into the house.

Jack winked at Regan and squeezed her hand. "Thanks, Ginny."

The Brewer sisters were at the kitchen table making a shopping list of ingredients they needed to prepare dinner.

"How does spaghetti sound to you two?" Fran asked.

"Great," Regan and Jack both answered.

"Super. We make a mean sauce," Fran said, pumping her fist.

"Now let's see," Ginny said. "It will be the four of us, maybe Skip, but I wouldn't hold my breath, and what about Dorie and Dan?"

"I don't think so," Regan answered. "They have a lot going on. But my best friend is joining us. She was in Boston on business. I invited her to come down and spend the night. As a matter of fact, she should be here by now."

"Oh," Ginny replied, devoid of enthusiasm. "Okay. What's her name?"

"Kit."

"Then that makes five of us, maybe Skip. Fran and I need a ride to the store. Neither of us drive in this weather." She looked at the FedEx box Jack had placed on the counter. "Regan, are you ever going to get around to opening that?"

"Yes I am, Ginny."

With Jack's help, Regan pulled the tabs off the cardboard box, then eased out the wrapped foiled package inside. A note was attached for Mr. and Mrs. Jack Reilly. "Oh," Regan said as she and Jack read the note together. "That's so nice."

"What's so nice?" Fran asked.

"My mother sent us the top layer of our wedding cake, which she froze after our wedding."

"Great!" Ginny answered. "We can have that for dessert."

"Ginny!" Fran protested. "We can't do that . . ."

Thank God, Regan thought.

". . . their anniversary isn't until Sunday," Fran continued. "We'll have it then."

"But it might go bad," Ginny said, practically. "It's already a year old."

Regan and Jack were standing behind the counter. Playfully, Jack stepped on her foot. Trying not to laugh, Regan started to speak. "Ginny, there's an old tradition that if a couple has a piece of their wedding cake on their first anniversary, it's supposed to bring them good luck."

"How should I know? The one guy I was supposed to marry decided he couldn't leave his mother. Remember, Fran?"

"Clear as a bell." Fran looked over at Regan and Jack. "Thirty years ago he told Ginny they'd get married after his mother died. So Ginny broke up with him. He passed over about five years ago, but his mother is still going strong."

"The woman is an ox," Ginny declared. "Through and through."

"That's too bad, Ginny," Regan said.

"Fran, as long as we're spilling secrets, tell what happened to you," Ginny instructed her sister.

"Oh Ginny, that's too sad."

"So what? This house has plenty of Kleenex."

"No."

"Go ahead. Jack and Regan are our friends."

"Oh . . ." Fran said. "Okay. When I was twenty-two my boyfriend asked my father for permission to marry me."

"Of course Daddy said yes," Ginny interrupted. "Fran's boyfriend was wonderful. Go on, Fran."

"I had no idea that had happened. My parents kept it a secret."

"I knew."

"That goes without saying, Ginny. Anyway, Robert had ordered the ring and was planning to propose on Saturday night. Saturday afternoon he went over to pick up the ring, but there was a bad accident . . ." Fran stopped speaking and shrugged her shoulders.

"Oh, Fran . . ." Regan said softly.

"Fran, we're so sorry," Jack said.

"Can you believe it?" Ginny asked indignantly. "She didn't even get to hear him propose. But his mother was a decent human being. She gave Fran the ring."

Fran nodded. "I wore it to Robert's funeral, then took it off and never wore it again. That ring is in a little red case in my jewelry box. I'll have it forever."

"So," Ginny said, taking a deep breath. "Those are our stories. Neither of us found anyone else. Not that we didn't try. *Oy vey.* Now we're grateful to have each other."

"We certainly are," Fran agreed.

"Both of you could still meet someone," Regan said encouragingly. "It's never too late."

"Regan, please!" Ginny protested. She started to laugh. "You know how hard it is to meet someone like Jack at our age?"

"At any age, Ginny. Believe me."

"Stop," Jack said, putting his hands up. "You're embarrassing me."

"You're adorable, Jack," Ginny said, then started giving instructions. "Regan, you'd better put that cake in the refrigerator."

"I will."

"Jack, could you drive us up to the market? We'll shop fast, I promise."

"Sure."

"I'll stay here and wait for Kit," Regan said. Not that I have a choice, she thought. Ginny wants Jack's undivided attention. I hope Lopez doesn't call him when they're in the car.

The sisters put on their coats and headed to the door. "Come on, Jack," Ginny called. "Regan, we'll be right back."

"Okay."

Jack leaned down and gave Regan a kiss. "See you later. Hold down the fort."

"I'll try."

As soon as they left, Regan dialed her mother.

Nora answered on the second ring. "Regan, how's everything?"

"Mom, thanks for the cake. You did some job wrapping it up."

"You're welcome. But tell me. Have you located Adele Hopkins's family?"

"Not yet," Regan said. "But we have her address in Chicago and Jack's in touch with the police out there."

"Then you should have no trouble finding them."

"The problem is, Mom," Regan said, "I don't think there's anyone to find."

49

Ellen hung Kit's saturated raincoat in the bathroom off the office, fished a clean pair of athletic socks out of her gym bag, and walked back to the showroom. Kit was sitting at the table, drying off her purse with a napkin. There was no one else in the store.

"Here, Kit," Ellen said, handing her the socks. "Take off those sneakers. Would you like coffee or tea?"

"Thank you so much. You don't have to go to all this trouble."

"No trouble. I'm glad you're here. What would you like?"

"A cup of tea would be great."

"Coming up."

Kit untied her sneakers, kicked them off, peeled off her wet thin socks, and stuffed them inside her shoes. After she pulled on the thick fluffy pair of athletic socks Ellen had been so thoughtful to lend her, Kit's feet felt like they might actually have a chance of thawing out. "Much better," she said to herself, then reached in her damp purse and dug out her cell phone. She pushed Regan's number and held the phone to her ear.

Four rings later, Regan answered. "Kit, I was starting to worry. Where are you?"

"Just when you thought things couldn't get any worse . . ."

"Oh, no," Regan said, laughing. "What happened?"

Kit explained.

"You're at Pillow Talk? How funny. Jack just left for the grocery store. When he gets back, I'll come get you. In the meantime, have Ellen tell you the story of why they started that shop."

"Regan, you don't have to come get me. I'm waiting to hear from the mechanic. Hopefully my car will be fixed soon. Besides, I know you're busy."

"I'm not going to let you walk through the pouring rain again. And I'm not that busy right now."

"What's going on with everything?"

Regan gave Kit a quick summary. "I'd like to update Ellen before we hang up."

"Okay. Just a minute, here she is." Kit held up the phone. "Ellen, Regan would like to talk to you."

Ellen placed a tray with a plate of cookies and a mug of hot tea in front of Kit, then took the phone from her. "Hi, Regan . . . Right . . . She lived in Chicago, huh? . . . We haven't heard back from the woman who sent that e-mail either . . . Keep me posted . . . Thanks." She handed the phone back to Kit.

"Hello again . . . Okay, Regan . . . sounds good . . . call me when Jack gets home." Kit closed her phone. "Regan says I should have you tell me why you started Pillow Talk."

Ellen's eyes twinkled. "You really want to know?"

"Yes."

"The restrained or unrestrained version?"

"Unrestrained, of course."

"I could tell. The way you laughed at my joke about Nathaniel Boone, I could tell. Pippy thinks I should tone down the way I talk about my ex-boss. But she's not here at the moment, so . . ."

"I'm all ears," Kit said as she poured milk in her tea. "Feel free to say whatever you want. Spare no details."

"Okay then," Ellen said with obvious delight. She sat at the table, placed her palms facedown, and looked Kit in the eye. "There I was, perfectly happy in my job selling makeup at a department store, when this complete moron walks up to my counter and tells me he wants to buy makeup for his mother. His mother!" She tilted her head, "You know that type of guy that . . ."

Within seconds, Kit was nodding in agreement.

50

Pippy drove along 5A for less than a minute before she switched on her left blinker, slowed down, and turned onto Woodsy Path, which Ellen said had been aptly named—aptly named, but hardly imaginative.

I love this street, Pippy thought as she drove slowly down the narrow, winding lane that was lined with overhanging trees. Each home along the way was shaded by evergreens, Roger's being the last house on the right. The road dead-ended with a large wooded area and pond. When she turned into her cousin's driveway, she shut off the car's engine. For a brief moment she sat, listening to the rain and taking in her surroundings. I'm going to hate to move, she thought. We've been here during the cold and dreary months and enjoyed it. I can just imagine how terrific it must be to live here in the summer.

She got out of the car, hurried to the front door, and let herself inside. The living room was to the left, the dining room to the right, the kitchen and den area straight ahead at the back of the house. A staircase to the three bedrooms was two steps away.

I hate to move out of here, but we definitely need more room, Pippy thought. The dining-room table was covered with every type of material, thread, and notion ever needed to make a pillow. Piles of sample pillows and boxes of cards they didn't have room for at the store filled the living room. Ellen and I are going to have to find a house with at least one big room where we can keep everything organized.

She walked down the tiny hallway, opened the basement door, and turned on the light. She started down the steps, but a sudden noise made her stop and wait for a moment. What was that? Nothing, she finally decided and kept going.

As soon as she reached the bottom step, she started a quick survey of the room. Everything looked okay. The three small windows were fine. No leaks, no drips, no broken glass. No water under the door that led to the backyard. Great, Pippy thought as she hurried back up the steps and shut the door.

The clock read 4:30. When we close the store at six, I'll go for that manicure, even though the weather stinks. After breaking that nail today, I definitely need it. She walked toward the kitchen, reached the island, then turned abruptly at a sound that seemed to come from upstairs. Her left elbow knocked over a glass vase filled with water, which started rolling off the counter. Pippy lunged for the vase, but it was too late. It dropped over the side of the counter and shattered on the tile floor.

I knew it! Pippy thought, angry with herself. This morning she'd thrown out the roses her parents had sent for her birthday a week ago, but she was in a rush. She'd left the vase on the counter, putting off washing it until after work.

Her heart racing, Pippy headed to the broom closet. No putting off that vase anymore, she thought as the wind rattled the front door.

51

Kit enjoyed every minute of Ellen's story. "Reed Danforth had no idea what was in store for him when he approached your makeup counter. At least for you, it led to your success," she said.

"But what if it hadn't?"

"He'd really be in trouble. Shh—Pippy's back."

"I knocked that vase over," Pippy cried as she hurried into the store. "That's why I took so long."

Ellen laughed and got up. She turned to Kit—"Do you need anything else?"

"No, I'll give Nathaniel Boone a call. I can't believe I haven't heard from him yet."

She dialed his number. After eight or nine rings, he answered. "Hello."

"Nathaniel?"

"Yes?"

"Nathaniel, this is Kit—I brought my car in earlier. My windshield wipers are broken . . ."

"I know. You told me."

"Have you had a chance to take a look under the hood yet?"

"No. I just fixed the other car good as new and feel quite

proud. I'll reward myself with a snack, then get started on your jalopy."

Broken windshield wipers do not a jalopy make, Kit thought. "Okay, great. Would you call me when you have an idea of how big the job is?"

"Every job's big. Every job's important . . ."

Meet Nathaniel Boone, the philosopher, Kit thought.

"From fixing the transmission, to changing a tire, it's all part of the whole. The whole car. A tire's no good if you don't have a transmission. A transmission's no good if you have a flat tire. Get it?"

"I get it. Let me know how long it will take, would you please?"

"Okay. Bye."

Kit exhaled, then called Regan.

"I wish I could come get you right now," Regan said. "Jack isn't back yet, which is surprising. They were only going to the market up the street. As soon as he gets here, I'll leave. It should be any minute."

"Thanks."

But it wasn't meant to be. The Brewers had asked Jack to take them to a specialty market three miles down the road for ingredients they couldn't find at the smaller grocery store. While they were shopping at the second store, a tree fell on a main road, blocking it completely. Their detour home would be lengthy.

At a quarter of six, Pippy and Ellen were closing the store. Jack wasn't home yet. Nathaniel Boone promised Kit's car would be ready soon. Who knew what that meant?

"Do either of you know the number of a local cab company? I'll go back and put the pressure on Boone."

"Pippy's going for a manicure," Ellen said. "Why don't you

come to the house with me, have a glass of wine, and as soon as the car is ready, I'll drive you over."

"Oh, Ellen, you don't have to do that."

"I want to. We'll have fun. I'm sure you have a story or two to tell me."

"You're a lifesaver."

"Hah! No one's ever called me that before!"

52

As time passed, Regan became restless. She got up several times from the couch, where she'd been reading and watching television, when she thought she heard Jack's car. She was anxious for Jack and the Brewers to return. So many thoughts were running through her head—if only I had a car to pick up Kit now. What would the news from Detective Lopez be? And how is Skip?

In the kitchen, she opened the drawer, found the Reillys' address book, looked up Skip's cell number, and called him. Fortunately, he answered. He didn't sound happy, but he answered.

"Hello."

"Skip, it's Regan. How are you?"

"Swell."

"Would you like to come to dinner?"

"No, thanks. I stopped by Fern's today. She told me to come back later at closing time. I'm friendly with a couple of her waitresses. We'll all have dinner."

"I'm glad to hear that."

"Whoop dee doo."

"Skip, please don't blame yourself."

"I'm trying. But it just happened this morning. I feel awful. You know how people say something hasn't set in yet?"

"Yes."

"I don't know how I could feel worse. If this hasn't set in yet, when it does, I'll end up in the loony bin."

"Oh, Skip. If there's anything I can do . . ."

"There's nothing anyone can do. I'm afraid to ask, but do you know anything about her family?"

"She was divorced last year and doesn't have kids. I'm sure we'll learn more before long."

"Regan?"

"Yes."

"Those apology cards . . . I keep thinking about that. Why were there so many? Who was she sending them to?

"Believe me, I've been wondering a lot about that myself."

"She mustn't have been as tough as she seemed."

"You're right, Skip. She probably wasn't."

He sighed.

"Skip, I hope we'll see you again over the weekend."

"I'm taking things a minute at a time. Besides," he said, his voice slightly amused, "aren't you and Jack supposed to be celebrating your anniversary? I brought in the breakfast food for you. Was everything okay?"

Regan hesitated. Should she tease him about the expired milk in the hopes he'd laugh? No, she decided. It's not worth the risk if it backfires.

"Was everything I brought okay?" he asked again.

"Yes. Everything was terrific."

"I'm glad."

"Skip, I'll give you a call tomorrow."

"Okay."

Regan closed her phone and walked over to the front window. At long last the reporter was gone.

Adele Hopkins will soon be yesterday's news.

53

This house is so pretty," Kit said as she and Ellen walked up Roger's front steps.

"I told Pippy we should look into squatters rights, but for some reason she was against it." Ellen unlocked the door and pushed it open. "Voilà!"

They stepped inside, and Ellen turned on the hall light. "Pretend you don't see anything to your left, and pretend you don't see anything to your right. Follow a straight line to the den. We have an excuse for these messy rooms, a business called Pillow Talk, but there are people out there who might consider us slobs."

"Not me."

"I didn't think so."

"But . . ."

"But what?" Ellen asked.

Kit's face looked earnest. "What about Reed Danforth? What would he think?"

Ellen chuckled. "You want me to start in on him again, don't you?"

"Yes."

"Good. I'll open the wine."

Kit followed her down the hall. "If my car isn't ready in the next hour, I'll have Regan pick me up. Jack should certainly be back by then."

"Fine. Take off your coat. There are hooks straight ahead by the back door. Red or white wine?"

"Red."

They both hung their coats. Kit placed her purse on a side table and pulled out her cell phone. She certainly didn't want to miss Nathaniel's call. She peered out the window of the back door. "Nice backyard. What's beyond those woods?"

"More woods. We're on Woodsy Path, remember?"

"How could I forget?"

Ellen poured the wine and handed a glass to Kit. "Cheers."

"Honestly, Ellen," Kit said as they clinked glasses. "I hope I get the chance to repay you in some way for being so hospitable to me today. And making me laugh so much."

An uninvited guest, well hidden, wanted to whisper in her ear, "You won't get the chance. She'll be dead."

"Don't worry about it," Ellen said with a wave of her hand. "I'm enjoying this. I'm not looking for . . ."

"I know you're not."

"Let's get comfortable."

The two of them sat on the couch.

Ellen took a sip of her wine, then placed her glass on the small coffee table. She frowned. "I can't think of his name. Who was it you wanted me to talk about?"

Kit grinned. "Reed Danforth," she answered as she placed the cell phone next to her.

"The lying lightweight Reed Danforth? Is that who you mean?"

Kit nodded.

"I thought so. I have a Danforth wish list. Would you like to know my first wish?"

"Of course."

"I'd like to round up all the women in Boston he hit on at makeup counters. I really would. Just to compare notes. Maybe ask a few questions."

"Like what?

"What was the state of his mother's health the day he appeared at your counter? Did he tell you he wanted to cheer her up, maybe with a new shade of *lipstick*?"

Kit laughed. "He must have been something."

"He was." Ellen sipped her wine. "Pippy says to forget him, and believe me, in most ways he's forgettable. You egg me on, Kit."

"Sorry. You're funny when you talk about him. Do you know what he's doing now?"

"No. Probably not much. I heard he has a girlfriend. She must have rocks in her head. Believe me, I'd like to have a boyfriend. But I'd never stoop that low. She must be desperate."

"You haven't heard from him at all since that first article was published?"

"No. What can he say? Everything I told that reporter is the truth. Kit, he asked me to leave a secure job, knowing that restaurant had a good chance of going down the tubes. They were already in debt because they'd spent so much money on that ridiculous renovation. If I had known that, I never would have quit my job. Then he doesn't even return my phone calls after they filed for bankruptcy!"

"You still haven't told me what he'd think about your front rooms."

Ellen laughed. "Kit, you are bad. Hmmm. What would Reed Danforth think . . . ? "

The unexpected guest's blood was boiling.

Ellen and Kit joked about Reed Danforth's possible reaction

to a variety of topics until Kit's cell phone rang twenty minutes later.

Kit put her glass on the table, reached for her phone, and quickly checked the caller ID. She answered. "Hi, Nathaniel."

"Hi. I'm proud to say your car is good as new. I'd really like to go home now."

"Thank you, Nathaniel. I'll be right there." She hung up, put the phone back down next to her, then reached for her glass. "The car is ready and Boone would like to go home." She took one last sip of wine.

"Let's go," Ellen said, walking over to the coat rack.

Ellen's wine glass was on the coffee table. Clearing her wine glass is the least I can do, Kit thought. She picked it up and carried both glasses to the counter.

Less than ten minutes later, Ellen pulled her car into Nathaniel's narrow driveway. Kit's car was parked in front of the garage.

"Ellen, thanks a million," Kit said, giving her a quick hug.

"Let's keep in touch."

"Absolutely."

Kit got out of the car and waved as Ellen pulled away. Nathaniel was inside the station, waiting on the folding chair.

"Hi, Nathaniel."

"Good as new," he said, handing her the bill.

His price seems fair, Kit thought. She put down her purse, got out her wallet, and handed him her credit card.

While he was processing the charge, she looked in her purse for her cell phone. She wanted to call Regan and tell her she was finally on the way. But the phone wasn't there. She kept looking. Did I leave the phone at Ellen's? Oh, no.

"May I have your autograph please?" Nathaniel asked.

Kit signed the receipt, thanked him, and was out the door. It was still pouring. She got in her car and started it. Holding her breath, she turned on the windshield wipers. They started to move. Kit smiled. Three seconds later they froze in place, wiping only the smile off Kit's face. Nathaniel was locking the glass door. She rolled down her window. "Nathaniel!" she yelled out to him.

"What?" he said, turning his head.

She pointed her finger. "Look!"

"Oh, no. I don't feel so proud anymore. First thing tomorrow morning, I'll find out what went wrong. I'd offer you a ride, but I walk to work. Two miles there and two miles back. Rain or shine."

"Don't worry about giving me a ride. But I do need to borrow your phone."

54

Regan and Jack were in the den, watching the evening news. Jack was unwinding after the ordeal getting home. Ginny and Fran were busy in the kitchen, slicing and dicing. They'd refused any help from Regan.

"I'm telling you, Regan," Ginny called out. "Jack has the patience of a saint. Sitting in all that traffic, the man never lost his cool."

"I know he does, Ginny," Regan answered, smiling at Jack and patting his leg.

Wearily, Jack smiled back, raising his eyebrows just a touch.

Regan's cell phone rang. "I hope this is Kit," she said, but after glancing at the caller ID, shook her head. "It must be someone from around here." She flipped open the phone. "Hello."

"Regan, it's Kit."

"Where are you calling from?"

"The station. My car isn't fixed, and I must have left my cell phone at Ellen and Pippy's house. Could you come get me?"

"Of course. Where is it exactly?"

Kit explained. "I'll wait in my car out front."

"Be right there." Regan hung up. She turned to Jack. "I'll be back in a few minutes."

"I'm coming with you."

"But you're barely out of the car."

"I missed you," he said softly.

Regan smiled. "I missed you too. Let's go."

They got up and walked to the kitchen. "We're going to get Kit. Her car isn't fixed," Regan explained.

Ginny's eyes widened. "Jack, you're going too? After all that traffic you were in today?"

"Yes, Ginny," Jack said as he put on his coat. "The weather is terrible. I don't want Regan driving alone."

"I suppose you're right."

As soon as they got in the car, Jack turned to Regan, smiled, then leaned over to kiss her. "Let's figure out the first weekend we don't have any plans and take that trip to Bermuda, okay?" he asked, stroking her hair.

Regan nodded. "More than okay."

They hugged for a moment, then Jack turned the key in the ignition.

It didn't take long to find Nathaniel's gas station. "I never noticed this place before," Regan said.

"Not much to notice," Jack answered as he turned into the driveway.

Kit got out of her car in an instant. "Alleluia!" she cried, waving her arms, then ran back to her trunk.

Regan and Jack both laughed. "I'll help her with her bags," Jack said. He put the car in park, stepped on the brake, and got out.

Regan watched as Jack gave Kit a kiss, then lifted her suitcase out of the trunk. I'm so lucky, she thought. I should really thank Dad more often for getting kidnapped.

A few moments later, after Jack transferred Kit's things from one trunk to another, Kit opened the back door. "Regan!" she exclaimed as she got in and shut the door.

"Kit, it's so good to see you," Regan said.

The two of them leaned between seats for a quick kiss on the cheek.

Jack opened the driver door and got in. "All set."

"I just have one request," Kit said.

"What?" Jack asked.

"That we make the briefest of stops at Pippy and Ellen's. It's on the way. I'm pretty sure I left my cell phone on their couch, but I can't call because Ellen's card only has the number of the shop."

"No problem," Jack said. "What street is it?"

"Woodsy Path."

"I remember passing that," Jack said as he shifted the car into drive.

"It's a cute block. Lots of trees and woods. Their house is charming but it's secluded at the end of the street. You know me, Regan. I'd be terrified to stay there alone."

55

Ellen pulled into Roger's driveway, turned off the engine, and got out. She opened the back door, reached down for her purse, and grabbed two plastic bags containing Chinese food she'd bought at a takeout place down the road from Nathaniel Boone's gas station. When Pippy got home, they'd heat up the food and have dinner together. She stepped back and pushed the door shut with her foot.

Will it ever stop raining? she wondered as she hurried up the walk. She went up the steps, unlocked the door, and stepped inside. As she was closing the door with her right shoulder, she could feel the bag in her left hand with the soup starting to give way. Quickly Ellen reached under the bag with her right hand so it wouldn't break. She still had the keys and the other plastic bag dangling from her fingers. These flimsy bags are such a joke, she thought as she ran down the hall to the kitchen. She reached the counter, carefully put the bag of soup down, dropped the keys, lifted the other bag onto the counter, and pulled off her shoulder bag. This Chinese food isn't even that good, she thought, as she caught her breath. Whew. She started walking toward the coat rack when something glistening on the floor caught her attention. She bent her knees, leaned over, and reached for it.

At that moment, a cord went around Ellen's neck. "Desperate?" a woman's voice snarled as she tightened the cord.

Ellen's left hand flew toward her neck as she frantically tried to get her fingers underneath the cord.

"You think I'm desperate? I'll show you who's desperate!" She tightened her grip.

Ellen lifted her right arm up over her head and swung it backwards.

"*Owwww!*" the woman screeched. Her grip on the cord loosened for a few seconds while she grabbed Ellen's right forearm.

Ellen quickly got her fingers around the cord and tried to pull. Thank you, Pippy, she thought. She doesn't have me yet.

The woman shook Ellen's arm. "Let go of whatever you have in your hand!" she screamed.

A shard of glass from Pippy's broken vase fell to the floor.

"*You miserable witch!*" she screamed as she tightened her grip on the cord again. "*You cut my face!*"

Ellen couldn't pull the cord away from her neck. It was choking her. She could barely breathe.

Jack turned into Roger's driveway. "This won't take long," Kit said. She got out and hurried to the front door. She was about to ring the bell when she heard screaming.

"*I hate you so much!*"

Oh my God, Kit thought. What's going on?

"*I hate you!*"

Kit put her hand on the door knob and realized the door wasn't completely shut. She pushed, and the door started to open. Kit's blood froze. Straight ahead of her she saw Ellen on the kitchen floor, a woman trying to strangle her. Kit turned toward the car and screamed, *"Regan! Jack! Help!"* then ran into the house, tore down the hallway, and jumped on the intruder.

"Get off!" Kit screamed, pummeling the woman with her fists.

"I love Reed Danforth. I am not desperate," the woman shrieked, blood running down her cheek.

Ellen tried to keep her grip on the cord with her left hand. She was struggling to breathe.

Kit slapped and punched Ellen's attacker, but the woman was so crazed she didn't seem to feel anything. She never stopped twisting the cord around Ellen's neck. Frantically, Kit turned, ran to the other side of the counter and started opening drawers in search of a knife. Jack and Regan came racing down the hall.

"I'm not desperate! Reed Danforth loves me!"

Jack lunged forward, "Let go!" he shouted, grabbing the assailant's wrists and squeezing so hard she screamed in pain. "Now!"

The maniacal woman howled, released her grip, and started sobbing. Jack stood over her while he called 911.

Regan and Kit ran to Ellen's side.

Ellen was holding her neck. Gulping for breath, she looked up at Kit. "I never expected you to return the favor this soon."

Kit smiled but her face was distraught. "Are you okay?"

"I'm great. It thrills me to think this psycho must be Reed Danforth's girlfriend. I'd like to get up . . ."

Regan and Kit helped her to her feet.

The "psycho" was sitting on the floor screaming and crying.

"Hey, you," Ellen said, breathing hard.

"What?" the woman snarled, then pointed to her bloody cheek. "Look what you did to me! Look!"

"Where's Reed?"

"*Boston!*"

"What I wouldn't pay to see his face when he hears about this," Ellen muttered.

"I'd like to take a quick look through the house before the police get here," Jack said. "We don't know what other lunacy she might have had in mind."

Regan nodded. "We have her covered."

Jack went upstairs and looked through the bedrooms. Then he came down the steps and went into the living room.

"It's so cluttered, I know" Ellen called.

"Don't worry about it," Jack said. "I just want to look around." He then walked through the dining room and the basement. When he came back into the den, he went over to the closet next to the fireplace.

"Hey, Jack," Ellen said.

Jack turned his head.

"That closet is so hard to open and close. It sticks like crazy. I doubt you'll find anything in there."

Jack shrugged. "I'll give it a try." He reached for the handle and pulled but nothing happened.

"See what I mean?"

Jack turned and smiled. "Let's try again." He yanked on the door hard. This time it did open. A man was crouched inside, looking miserable.

"*Reed Danforth!*" Ellen screamed. "Where's my camera? I want a picture for my website! I can't believe Pippy's not here!"

The "psycho" turned. A big smile spread across her face. "Darling! I missed you!" She jumped up and ran toward him, blood running down her cheek.

"Sit down," Jack ordered.

"Please Jack, just one picture. Just one," Ellen cried as her camera flashed. The "psycho" had reached the closet, turned, crouched down, and smiled. Her hand was on Reed's leg. "And one for safety," Ellen cried as her camera flashed again. "And one for good measure. Hey boss," she called to Reed, "where'd you meet your pretty girlfriend?"

"I bumped into him on the street!" Olivia squealed happily. "On purpose."

"Oh, how lovely," Ellen said, her voice dripping with sarcasm. "What goes around comes around. Don't you agree, Mr. Danforth?"

The sirens of police cars growing louder and louder filled Ellen with delight.

56

Jack's cell phone rang in the middle of a hubbub of police activity. He looked at the caller ID, then signaled to Regan. "Lopez," he mouthed, pointing to his phone, then pointed upstairs.

Regan nodded.

They went upstairs to one of the bedrooms and shut the door.

". . . Now we're in a quiet room," Jack told Lopez. "Do you mind if I put you on speakerphone? . . . great . . ." Jack flipped a switch on his phone. "Okay, what do you have?" he asked.

"I have the name and number of the ex-husband. He lives two hours outside of Chicago on an estate. Loves the role of the country gentleman. The concierge was sending Hopkins's mail to a PO box in Boston. He and Hopkins were friendly, and she told him she'd been married to her ex for ten years but never talked about her earlier life, and he felt uncomfortable asking. The name of her ex is Randolph Windwood. Hopkins said Windwood was born into too much money. Nothing else, really."

"Randolph Windwood is his name?"

"Yes, and his number is . . ."

Regan wrote it down.

"Okay. We'll take it from there. Thanks so much. I appreciate your help." Jack hung up the phone.

"This is great," Regan said. "Her ex-husband might not be 'Mr. Wonderful,' but he must have some information for us. You want to call now?"

"Yes, I do." Jack opened his phone again and started pushing in the number. "Let's give Randolph a shout."

After four rings, a man answered. "Windwood Residence."

"Hello," Jack said. "I'd like to speak to Randolph Windwood, please."

"Who is calling?"

"My name is Jack Reilly. I'm a captain with the NYPD. I'm calling to inquire about Adele Hopkins."

"Please hold."

"I think that was the butler," Jack whispered, as he held the phone out so Regan could listen.

"Hello. Randolph Windwood on the line."

Windwood sounds so affected, Regan thought, as Jack introduced himself.

"What do you want to know about Adele?"

"She had an accident this morning. Her body was swept out to sea, and we're trying to find her family."

"Oh dear. Before our divorce, she only had me. No more."

"We knew she didn't have children, but isn't there anyone?"

"No parents, no siblings, no children. She has dreary cousins somewhere, but I was never interested in seeing them. I have no idea where they are now."

"Perhaps you could give us the names of a few of her friends."

"When she married me, she started a new life. We socialized with my friends. Though none of them really took to her. Doesn't matter now. Where was the accident?"

"Cape Cod."

"Cape Cod!" Randolph started laughing and laughing. "My word, how amusing."

"Why?"

"Maybe you should be talking to her first husband."

"Her first husband?"

"Yes. Adele was married for more than twenty-five years to this fellow. I always suspected that after the initial excitement of our marriage, the horsey set wasn't for Adele, and she missed her old life. What a difficult woman. So, so difficult. She left that man for me, you know. Maybe she was trying to reignite the flame by moving back. He was a teacher."

"Where does he live?"

"Long Branch, Massachusetts. One of those small folksy towns that have never interested me. I don't want to look out my window and see children riding bicycles down the street. I'd rather see horses running through the fields. My children rode horses. I don't think either of my daughters ever rode a bicycle come to think of it."

"You have children?"

"Yes, and just last year my first grandchild."

"Congratulations," Jack said, making a face at Regan, while she rubbed her fingers together, nodded her head, and mouthed the word "money." "Mr. Windwood, would you please tell me the name of Adele's first husband?"

"Why not? He might know where some of those cousins reside. He's the type to keep in touch with all the bores. When I first met Adele she told me she made a new photo album each year of all her students. Why on earth would you do that I asked? You'll never want to look at their pictures again. I think she and that husband were born with a certain gene that enabled them to derive pleasure from matters I find most tedious."

"Adele was a teacher?"

"Yes. She taught the eighth grade."

"I'm curious," Jack said. "You don't sound as if you had that much in common. How did you and Adele meet?"

"Adele's father was dying. She took a leave of absence and went home to Oregon to be with him at the hospital. Her mother had died the year before. She had no siblings. I was also in the hospital, the result of a bad riding accident from which I have fully recovered. Mr. Hopkins's room was right next door to my private room. His wasn't private, but, well, what can you do? Anyway, we met three or four days after she arrived. Adele was asked to wait in the hallway when her father's doctor came in to do whatever doctors do when they zip those curtains around the bed. I looked out, and there she was looking so sad. For some strange reason I'll never understand for the life of me, I waved. She waved back. We chatted. Next thing you know, she's spending time in my room while her father slept, getting me tea, trying to make me comfortable. We fell in love, and she never went back to what's his name."

"What *is* his name?"

"Jimmy Cannon. I think that he and many others in that little town were quite angry with Adele."

"We'll try and get in touch with him."

"It's a shame about Adele. If you find any relatives, please give them my condolences. No wait. Tell them to enjoy my money. Adele got quite a nice settlement. So long now."

Jack closed his phone. "Wow."

"Wouldn't want to be married to him," Regan said.

Jack smiled. "Let's see if there's a listing for Cannon." He dialed information. There was a James Cannon in Long Branch, Massachusetts, but the number was unlisted. He flipped his phone shut. "We'd better get back downstairs. Tomorrow morning let's take a drive to Long Branch. Cannon shouldn't be too hard to find in a small town. I just hope he'll be willing to talk to us."

"Jack, the slashed pillow was postmarked in Long Branch."

"I know. But if Cannon *is* willing to talk, I'm sure it will be interesting."

57

Devon was feeling on top of the world as he drove his little group back to The Castle by the Sea. They'd had a wonderful Italian dinner together. They'd laughed and talked. Everyone's favorite topic was themself, naturally. But for Devon, what was most exciting was the way they all raved about the faux knife. *Ah, to think how nervous I was. Tomorrow night's cocktail party should be quite exciting, the highlight being the reading, of course.*

He pulled the car down the driveway of The Castle.

"Great dinner, Devon."

"Loved the spaghetti."

"What most impressed me was the knife," said Annie, the little ingénue who could be most annoying. "Not only is it an amazing fake knife, but I have such respect for the way you handled the situation."

Devon nodded his head.

"Wait till Floyd sees that knife," Hadley Wilder said. "He will be amazed. How can he not be? It looks so real. The handle is gorgeous."

Devon was glowing when he parked the car. He'd been smiling to himself while the others headed inside. No one noticed he was still sitting in the driver's seat. Oh well. Must be a sign. I've been mulling this course of action all night, and now the decision has been made for me. Cheerily, he turned the car back on and headed to Floyd's.

"I love the theatre," Devon sang to himself. "Floyd will love the knife, um hmm hmm, la la la."

Slowly, he turned onto the narrow beach road that ended in front of the house he had rented for Floyd. There were only three houses on the street. I don't want to get too close, in case I decide not to ring the bell and have to make a fast getaway. Devon parked next to an overgrown thicket of bushes, grabbed the knife, his umbrella, and went out the door.

He probably won't invite me in, Devon thought as he walked toward Floyd's, trying to avoid puddles. Can't say I blame him. But I would like for him to have just one little peek at this beautiful prop.

The lights are on. Lovely! With a big smile, Devon walked across Floyd's driveway and toward the walkway, mindless of the rain. The curtains were all closed, which was not surprising. He continued up the walkway, then hesitated. Is that yelling I hear? Inching closer until he was on the porch with his head cocked, Devon realized what he was hearing were lines from his play! Floyd was rehearsing—with a woman!

He is some devil. Of course I can't interrupt. But it would be nice to hear what his process is when he works with someone else. This person must be someone Floyd respects. I'd be able to hear more if it were a nice quiet evening instead of all this drip drip drip. He listened intently. Hmmm. Whoever the woman is doesn't sound as if she's trained in theater. No, the poor dear, not at all. Maybe it's someone he's dating.

Devon turned. No knife presentation tonight. He went down the steps and stopped. Floyd had just yelled something that was not a line from his play. Oh, well. Every word of his mouth can't be a line from my play. Devon took a step, and Floyd yelled again. He sounds a little crabby.

I'd better get out of here. If he's crabby, the last thing I want is for him to find me eavesdropping. That would be frightfully embarrassing.

Picking up the pace, Devon hurried back to his car. Who is she? Devon wondered. Did he bring her up from New York?

Oh well, that's his business.

Tomorrow night I will show him the knife before we begin. Exactly when, I don't know.

Saturday, April 8th

58

On Saturday morning, Regan and Jack snuck out of the house before anyone else was up. Kit knew where they were going. So did Ginny and Fran.

Adele Hopkins had been alone in the world. If her first husband could give them the name of a distant cousin, someone who cared about Adele, they'd be grateful.

One hour and fifteen minutes after they left, Regan and Jack were driving down Main Street in Long Branch, headed for Washington Middle School. They'd done some research online the previous night and learned that Jimmy Cannon still worked there as a teacher and coach.

They found the school, parked, and went out to the athletic field, where a soccer game was about to begin.

Jack and Regan walked over to one of the coaches.

"Quick question," Jack said. "Do you know where I can find Jimmy Cannon?"

The coach pointed. "His house is right across the street from the field. Which is perfect for him."

"Do you know if he'd be home now?"

"Probably. His team plays this afternoon."

"I hear he's a nice guy."

"Salt of the earth. But to be honest, he's really down in the dumps. He's getting divorced, which is good because his wife is a shrew. But it's his second divorce. Not easy."

"That's tough. Which house?"

"The blue one."

Regan and Jack rang the bell. A big teddy bear of a man answered the door. He had brown hair graying at the temples, brown eyes, a sprinkling of freckles across his nose, and was wearing a sweatsuit.

He does look sad, Regan thought.

"Can I help you?"

"I hope so, but you might not want to. My family has a house on Cape Cod. Adele Hopkins was renting the house next door."

"Adele?"

A light came into his eyes, Regan thought. He still cares, at least a little. This guy didn't slash any pillow.

"Yes. But she had an accident yesterday"

"Oh." The flicker in his eyes disappeared.

"The people who rented her the house have no idea who to contact. We thought you might know of other family members."

"Not really, but come on in."

They sat with him in his living room and told him what they knew about Adele.

"Everybody thought it was awful what she did to me," Jimmy said. "Which is natural. But I also blame myself. She was out there at the hospital with her dying father, day in and day out. There was no one to share the burden. I was too busy coaching to take any time off. I flew out there with her for the first few days, then left. Never came back. We were together since college. We weren't blessed with kids, but we had each other. What did I expect? I should have been there for her."

"It's a shame," Jack said. "Her marriage to Windwood wasn't happy."

"You mean Windbag?"

They all laughed.

"That's exactly who I mean," Jack said.

"We found apology cards on Adele's dining room table," Regan said. "I think she was filled with regret."

"Apology cards?"

"Yes. She didn't by any chance send you a decorative pillow did she?" Regan asked.

"Maybe she did. The woman I'm divorcing went through all my mail, my cell phone. It was crazy. I have nothing to hide."

"When did you separate?" Regan asked.

"A month ago."

Jack and Regan looked at each other, then told him about the slashed pillow postmarked Long Branch.

"What?" He folded his arms and shook his head. "I'll have to remember that if I ever have second thoughts. I'm sorry. I would have liked to talk to Adele. GRUDGE ME, GRUDGE ME NOT. She was funny, she really was. On our first date, we went rowing in a park, and she was standing up in the boat and giggling. We were eighteen." He exhaled. "What can you do?"

"Adele had a little rowboat on Cape Cod. She was out there in all kinds of weather," Regan told him.

"She did? When we were married, we never went rowing. We were too busy with coaching the kids' teams. And Windbag's estate doesn't sound like a place you'd row. Well, maybe he had a lake. I don't know." His voice trailed off.

"So you don't know any relatives we can call?"

"I don't. I can look through old address books in the attic."

"Don't worry about it," Jack said. "We were really hoping to find someone out there who loved Adele Hopkins."

We just did, Regan thought.

59

———◆———

"Hello strangers!" Ginny called. "We're in the den."

It was too much to hope that Jack and I would ever spend time in this house alone, Regan thought, as she and Jack walked into the kitchen.

"How are you Ginny?" Jack asked.

"Better now."

"Fran?"

"Good. We're sitting here reading about you in the paper. You saved that girl's life. Ellen's lucky Kit forgot her cell phone, huh?"

"She is," Jack agreed.

"Well thanks to your heroics," Ginny said. "We're all invited to the cocktail party at The Castle by the Sea tonight."

"What's the occasion?" Regan asked.

"A traveling theater group just hit town. They're performing a play under a tent at The Castle for a month, starting Memorial Day. They'll read one scene at the party, hopefully not for long, and then everyone can go back to having a good time. Six o'clock to eight o'clock. We should leave here by 5:45."

"Who invited us?"

"The director himself."

"What's the play?"

"Grandpa, Go Home."

I'm not going near that one, Regan thought. "Sounds good."

"Eh, we'll see."

"Where's Kit?"

"She took a cab to Pillow Talk. I can't believe Kit and Ellen were making fun of Ellen's old boss, and there he was, locked in the closet!" Ginny exclaimed.

"Did Kit tell you that?"

"No. It's on the front page of the paper."

"What about Dorie and Dan?" Regan asked.

"Haven't heard a peep out of them."

"Maybe they'd like to come to the party."

"Sure, invite them. The more the merrier."

Not always, Regan thought.

60

A*dele* you have inspired me."

"That's good."

"I will never act again with a fake weapon. Those prop knives drain the lifeblood of an actor. It's insulting. We're not children playing a game of cops and robbers. I never thought of it that way, Adele. We're doing *Theater!* I cannot wait to perform this evening. Your eyes look a little droopy. Did you have a good rest last night?"

"Tied to a chair?"

"Oh yes. It would be better if the chair had a cushion." Floyd picked up his script. "Time to do lines."

"I just need to put my head down for a minute."

"Are you crazy? We must rehearse!" He picked up his script from the chair. "Tonight I must shine!" he said as he turned the pages. A funny noise made him look up.

Adele was asleep on the couch. Even worse, she was snoring.

"You can't do this to me, Adele. Wake up!"

Slowly she opened her eyes.

"There you go."

She tried to sit up, but the effort was too great. She fell back and was out cold.

61

At quarter to six, Ginny opened the front door of the Reilly home. "Ready to go, everybody?" she called out. "Fran and I will wait in the car."

"We're all ready," Regan answered from the hallway where she'd been standing by Kit's bedroom door, chatting as Kit put on her makeup.

Kit spritzed herself with perfume. "Ready. Should I take my car, Regan? I'm so happy it's finally fixed."

"No. Don't be silly. We'll all ride together."

"Okay. I'll be leaving first thing in the morning."

"Please. Stay as long as you want."

Jack came out of the bedroom. "We're all set. Dan and Dorie will meet us there?"

"Yes," Regan answered. "I'm glad they're coming. Dan really wanted to stay home because of something about work but Dorie insisted. I still can't believe they found Adele's plaque under the bed."

"What was it?" Kit asked.

"A Favorite Teacher—Favorite Coach award for Adele Cannon. Washington Middle School."

"Wow," Kit said. "That's sad."

They started walking down the hall. "Pippy and Ellen will be at the party," Kit mentioned.

"Even Skip is going to make it," Regan said. "I think Fern insisted he join her. Whatever it takes. I hate to think of him sitting home alone."

The five of them rode over, Regan and Jack in the front, Kit squeezed in the middle in the back between Ginny and Fran.

"Look how gorgeous!" Ginny cried as The Castle by the Sea came into view. "Look at the sky." Above the castle, the sky was streaked with blues and reds and purples. "The sun's finally trying to come out. I bet tomorrow will be a beautiful day."

Jack started to turn where a sign indicated parking. "Wait Jack," Ginny said. "We have VIP parking."

"We do?"

"After I thanked the director for inviting us, I inquired about parking. When he told me, I asked if there was anything closer because I have a bum knee."

"You do?" Regan asked sympathetically.

"No. Jack, pull down the driveway. We'll go in through the kitchen."

In the kitchen, trays of cold hors d'oeuvres were ready to be passed. Hot hors d'oeuvres were heating in the oven. Devon was having a quick chat with the caterer when Ginny knocked on the door.

Devon answered. "Welcome."

"I'm the one you spoke to on the phone," Ginny said. "Here are Regan and Jack Reilly . . ."

They stepped inside and introductions were made.

Devon had been a nervous wreck all day. Then the press conference was a disaster. Only one reporter showed up, and he was late. All he wanted to talk about was Adele Hopkins, making the cast even more dispirited. Did they realize she had drowned so close by? Do they think of her as a tragic figure? . . . Devon had cut the reporter off and tried to put Adele Hopkins out of his own mind. It was difficult, but the show must go on. "Hello, hello everyone," he said, then turned to Regan, Jack, and Kit. "Your quick action last night saved that woman's life. You are to be commended."

"We did what anyone would have done," Jack said.

"I'm just glad I forgot my cell phone."

"Indeed. It's frightening how many crazy people there are out there. Ah, well. Please, go inside and enjoy."

In the grand parlor, the mood was festive. Two bars were set up at either end of the room, and waiters were also passing around drinks. Before long Pippy and Ellen and Dan and Dorie joined the Reillys' group. Skip and Fern and a young girl arrived and walked toward them. Regan realized that the girl was the waitress from Fern's she and Jack had met yesterday.

"Hi," Regan said. She gave Skip a kiss on the cheek. "I'm so glad you're here."

"Thanks," he said with a shrug. "Have you met Lila?"

"Yesterday. She took good care of us at Fern's."

Lila smiled.

"She took good care of us too," Dorie said, waving her glass. "Last November. It was one of the first days that you were on the job."

What a day that was, Dan thought.

"Of course," Lila said. "You told me you had a house on Pond Road and came to Fern's often during the summer. I remember everything about those first few days. I was so nervous." She laughed. "I kept a diary, and it's funny to read now. That woman you walked out with was nice, but I think I annoyed her

250

because I talked too much. I asked her about her omelette. Was it well done enough? Are you sure? I felt so bad. I did everything wrong."

"Lila, you're a great waitress," Fern said.

"I'm just glad you weren't there that day."

Fern laughed.

Dorie wasn't going to tell her, but she couldn't resist. "That woman we walked out with was Adele Hopkins. The woman who drowned."

Lila's mouth dropped. "She was?"

Skip's face fell.

You're killing me, Dorie, Dan thought.

Poor Skip, Regan thought. Poor Skip.

"May I introduce myself?" a man's voice boomed.

Yes, Regan thought, please.

They all turned their attention to the attractive, charming man with white hair and a commanding presence. He was clearly a member of the cast.

"I know you," Fern laughed.

"Fern knows everybody." Jack said.

"And I was the one who took care of you when you bought all that food yesterday, Lila said eagerly. "The cheeseburger, the omelette, the . . ."

"Yes, you did," Floyd interrupted. "To you others who I have not met, I just want to say hello. My name is Floyd Wellington, and I am in the play. I hope you enjoy yourselves." He turned and started to mingle with other guests.

Ellen stopped him. "I met you in New York City way back when at the stage door and you were so nice to me . . ."

Finally it was time for the reading. Devon hadn't told Floyd he couldn't use his knife. He'd waited until the eleventh hour, then Floyd was so annoyed after the press conference, Devon opted for the cowardly way out. He'd seen Floyd put his knife inside his script, then place it on his chair. Devon had switched knives without telling him. Floyd would act like a pro, he thought. If he gets mad, he can yell at me later.

"May I have everyone's attention?" Devon asked. The crowd quieted. "I am so pleased you joined the Traveling Thespians tonight . . ." He then went on for a few minutes about his play and how wonderful it was to be on Cape Cod. "And now I'd like to introduce my actors," he said. One by one they came out and took their places. "Ladies and gentlemen," Devon said. "I hope you enjoy this scene from *Grandpa, Go Home.*"

The actors opened their scripts.

Devon eagerly watched for Floyd's reaction. He might get annoyed but he'll have to realize how incredibly real this knife looked. But when Floyd opened his script, Devon's knees went weak. A dark fury enveloped Floyd's face. It was unlike anything Devon had ever seen. When Floyd started to say his lines, he delivered them with such anger, no one laughed.

For ten torturous minutes, the crowd watched as Floyd waved around the fake knife, looking as if he wanted to kill someone instead of like a grandpa proud of the gift he'd brought his family.

When the scene ended, the crowd politely clapped.

Ginny rolled her eyes. "Looks like a real winner."

When the actors exited, Devon went running after Floyd, who was obviously leaving. Floyd was muttering to himself. "Kill you . . . You convinced me . . . I looked like a fool . . . couldn't act without my knife . . . I'm going to *KILL* you . . ."

Devon grabbed Floyd's arm.

Floyd turned around. He was wild-eyed with rage. He wiped his face with his hand, still muttering to himself. Then he turned and took off.

Did he say he wants to kill someone? Devon wondered. He ran back into the reception where people tried to falsely congratulate him, but he ignored them and hurried over to Regan and Jack's group. They all looked at him.

"I'm sorry," he said to Jack. "Floyd just left. I know there's a woman at his house. He didn't tell me. I stopped by last night and heard him rehearsing with someone so I didn't ring the bell. He's a little crazy, and now he's furious. The way he delivered his lines tonight was insane. He's never read them like that before. Just now, I tried to speak to him. He was muttering about killing someone. I think he's losing his mind. He ran out of here in a frenzy. It might be silly but *please* . . . Can you take a run over there? Maybe if you just check . . ."

"Where does he live?" Jack asked Devon.

"Right on the beach a little ways down from here."

"I know," Skip said. "The real estate agent paid me to leave food for him at his house."

"Come with us," Jack said quickly.

Jack, Regan, and Skip ran for the door. They raced through the kitchen and out to Jack's car.

"Take a right at the end of the driveway," Skip said frantically as Jack started the car. "It's not far at all."

"We can't just barge in there," Jack warned. "He's angry, but we don't know he's done anything wrong."

They reached Floyd's street. Jack zoomed around the corner, down to Floyd's house. A car was in the driveway, the lights still on, the driver door wide open.

"Oh boy," Jack said as they got out of the car and ran up the walk. They reached the steps when they heard Wellington scream, *"I'm going to kill you. You made me look like a fool!"*

"There's a key," Skip said, lifting up a plant. His hand was trembling as he reached down and handed it to Jack. *"I'm going to kill you now!"* Quickly Jack opened the door. Wellington came running out of the kitchen, waving a knife, and charged down the basement steps. Jack raced down the steps after him, grabbed his right arm, and tackled him. Together they fell down the last three steps.

"Jack!" Regan screamed. Wellington was face down, trying to get up. Jack was on top of him. Jack pressed down on Wellington's shoulders with his hands, and kneed him in the back. Regan stepped on Floyd's arm.

"He's pretty strong," Jack said. "No drama please, Floyd. Let go of the knife."

Floyd released his grip. *"Oh! Woe is me!"* he cried.

Regan carefully picked the knife up off the floor.

Skip had so much wanted to help. He was right behind Regan, but everything happened so fast. He was standing on the bottom step. Music was blaring. The basement was dark, but in the light from the stairway, he could see a woman across the room tied to a chair. He hopped over Wellington's legs and found a cord for the overhead light. A bare bulb lit the room. He turned to the woman.

"Mrs. Hopkins!" he screamed. He ran over, leaned down, and put his arms around her. "Mrs. Hopkins," he said, starting to cry. "I'm so glad you're alive."

"I am too." Adele buried her face in his jacket. Tears were spilling from her eyes. "I am too," she sobbed.

Sunday, April 9th

62

The next morning Regan and Jack were sleeping, Jack's arm around Regan's side, when they were awakened by a loud knocking at their bedroom door.

Regan turned toward Jack.

"I don't want to disturb you, but we're leaving," Ginny called.

"Am I dreaming?" Regan whispered.

Jack's eyes were sleepy. He shrugged, then cleared his throat. "You're leaving?" he called.

"Yes. We wanted you to have peace and quiet on your anniversary. Fran and I are going up to Boston to visit a friend and spend the night. It's a gorgeous day, and we want to get going. It's already 8:30."

"If you give us a few minutes, we'll come out and say good-bye," Jack told her.

"Great!"

Jack smiled at Regan, then put his head on her shoulder. "This is worth getting up for," he whispered.

When they came out, Fran and Ginny were standing in the living room.

"Happy Anniversary!" Fran said.

"You're up early," Jack said, "especially after all the excitement last night."

"I still can't get over it," Ginny declared. "It's so wonderful. Skip is a new man." Is that actor a nut or what?"

"He's a nut," Regan agreed.

"And Adele Hopkins is still alive? Unbelievable. She was right under our noses."

They all hugged and kissed goodbye, then Ginny and Fran left.

When the door shut, Jack shook his head. "That's really surprising."

"I wouldn't have predicted it," Regan said. "I'll make coffee."

Kit came out and joined them for breakfast. "Happy Anniversary. I'll have a cup of coffee, and then I'm hitting the road."

Naturally they rehashed the events of the previous evening.

". . . and what I can't get over is that the expired milk came from that house!" Regan said. "Skip bought groceries for us and that nut job Floyd at the same time. He went to Floyd's house first, started unpacking the bags, then opened the refrigerator and realized he better clean it out. Everything was on the counter and got mixed up." She laughed. "I feel so much better that mystery is solved."

When Kit left, Jack went to buy the papers. Regan opened all the windows. The sun was shining, and life was good. She smiled at the thought of Adele's face when Jimmy Cannon walked in last night. Jack had called him minutes after they found her.

When Jack returned, they read the papers, then went for a long walk on the beach. It felt great to be out in the sunshine. They ran into Dan and were introduced to his boss who'd come down for the day. They'd been strolling along, deep in discussion, obviously enjoying themselves.

At 5:30 they left the house. Jack was wearing a jacket and tie, Regan a cocktail dress.

The restaurant was elegant but stuffy. Everyone spoke in hushed serious tones. The floorboards creaked as they followed the hostess to their table. But the food was delicious. They refused dessert.

"We have to go home and have that wedding cake or my mother will be very disappointed," Regan said.

Driving home, as they were passing Ginny and Fran's house, Jack said, "Regan, I think we have the whole block to ourselves. Dan and Dorie left."

"Unbelievable."

Jack parked the car, and they got out.

"Will you look at that full moon?" Jack asked as he came around to take Regan's hand. They were standing at the back of the car. "It's such a beautiful night. I think I'd like to ask my wife to dance with me in the moonlight. It is our first anniversary, after all." He looked down at her.

Regan smiled. "Let's dance."

He led her to the end of the driveway, took her in his arms, and they started slow dancing. "My love," Jack sang, "there's only you in my life . . ." Regan joined him in song. They laughed at how bad they sounded but it didn't stop them. "My Endless Love" was followed by "Just the Way You Look Tonight" and "Till There Was You" . . .

"Okay," Jack finally said. "I've made a decision. Every year on our anniversary, I'm going to carry you over the threshold." He scooped Regan up and then twirled her around. They were both giddy. As he started up the walk, Regan tapped him on the shoulder. Jack stopped and looked down. "Pardon me, boy?" she sang. "Is that the Chattanooga choo choo?"

"Oooh, oooh, oooh" Jack sang. "Dah, dah, dah, dah." He

twirled her around again. "Is that the Chattanooga choo choo?" he sang as he carried her up the steps.

He put the key in the door, pushed it open, and carried Regan over the threshold. "Alone at last!" he cried, then flicked on the light.

"*Surprise!*" Ginny, Fran, Kit, Pippy, Ellen, Nora, Luke, Eileen, Dennis, Adele and Jimmy, Skip, Lila, Fern, Dorie, Dan, Mickey McPhee, Devon and his cast were standing in the living room.

Ginny came running over. "I wanted to go out there and cut in. I hope you don't mind, but we all wanted to celebrate with you tonight. What a crazy weekend it's been! We figured you wouldn't mind one more surprise. You have so many people who love you!"

Regan and Jack were smiling as he put her down.

"We don't mind, do we Regan?"

"No. I don't think Devon will ever hire us to be in any of his musicals . . ."

"You have potential!" Devon assured them.

Everyone laughed.

While they were laughing, Ginny whispered to Regan. "Adele comes back from the dead and lands a man one-two-three." She rolled her eyes. "What am I doing wrong?"

"A few lessons is all it takes," Devon continued.

"I must say," Jack said. "We *never* suspected this."

"Not in the least," Regan agreed.

Kit handed them glasses of champagne. Under her breath she said, "Ginny's idea."

"It's fine," Regan said.

Adele Hopkins raised her glass. "Regan and Jack. Thank you for giving me my life back. In more ways than one." Jimmy's arm was around Adele. He kissed her on the top of her head. They looked like they belonged together.

Regan and Jack held up their glasses. "We couldn't be happier for you," Regan said.

"Hear, hear," Devon cried.

The crowd echoed his words and sipped their Champagne.

Ellen came forward holding a gift box. "Thank you both," she said. "If not for you, I wouldn't be here. I made you a pillow embroidered with a sentiment that I thought would be perfect for your anniversary. I know it's what everyone in this room wishes for you." She pulled the top off the box and held it out for them to see.

Regan smiled. "That is perfect."

"Thank you, Ellen," Jack said, then looked down at Regan. "It's my fondest hope."

"Mine too." Regan turned and gazed back at the words:

MAY YOU GROW OLD ON ONE PILLOW